Return with Honor

Jane Carver

Published by
Satin Romance
An Imprint of Melange Books, LLC
White Bear Lake, MN 55110
www.satinromance.com

ISBN: 978-1-61235-463-7

Published in the United States of America.

Cover Art by: Caroline Andrus

Dedicated to Nancy Schumacher, owner and manager of Melange-books.com. She and her staff help writers with good stories become writers with even better ones. I'm a better writer, a better author, for being part of her world.

Acknowledgements:

Annette Long-Stinnett, Special Assistant
Community Services Group
Cherokee First

H H Self
Baca County, CO Emergency Management Director/EMT/Firefighter
Medical information

Criminal Investigation—Ronald F. Becker
An Aspen Publication 2000

Chapter One

Jud Longtree had the oddest feeling his life was about to change when a black-haired beauty passed him in a dead out run, headed toward two young men who'd just emerged from the door of a shop further up the sidewalk. From the looks of the two so intent on fighting, they wouldn't even see her until one of them knocked her flat. Better to break up the fight than see the lady suffer. So he lengthened his stride and got to them as the first one took a swing.

His thought was to step between the guys and force the weaker one away. Less than thirty seconds into the melee, he realized that both knew how to box as well as wrestle. Jud ducked as a fist the size of a small ham swung at the light-haired shorter teen, missed and came straight for his jaw. His body swayed to one side, close but out of the line of contact.

The two ducked and swung, contacted, grunted and cursed fluently. The taller, but more slender boy got the other in a headlock and proceeded to batter his opponent's head until blood leaked out of the visible ear.

The one in the weaker position jabbed the taller boy in the kidneys, each blow accompanied by bellows of fury. "Let go, Peter!"

"Quit arguing with me then, damn it!" Another blow caught him in the ribs. "Ow, Walter!"

While Jud stood back, now hesitant to interfere in local affairs, the woman had moved to the other side of the fighters, and she looked determined to break up the two. With those wide eyes, forehead

1

wrinkled in worry and tight straight lips, she appeared as angry as the combatants. "Shit, this is gonna get ugly," he muttered in dismay as she yelled at him.

"You knock them apart, and take Peter." She pointed to the taller thinner boy. "I'll take care of Walter," she said, pointing to the one in the headlock.

"Are you crazy?" He could imagine her wading in between them like an eager puppy, ready to play, and being seriously injured. He wouldn't let one of his men in Iraq do something like that, and he wasn't about to let her either.

She had other ideas. "On my count." She literally rolled up her sleeves and began a loud quick countdown. "One. Two. Three."

Jud figured he had no choice. Help or pick up the pieces. Her willingness to become involved fascinated him at the same time it annoyed him. As she yelled *three* and pulled her shoulders back, he dug in his heels and tackled the taller boy. He and Peter went over, Jud landing on top, his weight heavy enough to break the boy's concentration.

"Hey, mister, what the hell are you doing?" Peter tried to throw Jud off, but he flipped the kid over onto his stomach, caught both hands and held them in a tight grip. Other than his mouth—he cussed like a Marine—the rest of the kid was down for the count.

Jud looked for the woman just in time to see the boy she called Walter fly through the air. Tall, dark and beautiful had just thrown him over her hip in a classic martial arts move. The kid landed on his stomach, not four feet from Jud. Before he could whistle his appreciation, she ran over, put her knee in the kid's back, caught his thumb and bent it back. A gurgling scream rumbled out of the boy's throat, but he didn't move.

"High five, big guy." Sweaty, with a breathy grin, she held up one hand, palm out to Jud, and waited for him to join her celebration.

He shook his head and grimaced, unprepared to share her victory. She was as crazy as the two kids lying on the sidewalk. Besides, they had attracted a crowd, and this was not how he wanted to meet the folks of Bleaker, South Carolina, again. Seemed he had no choice though. He ignored the woman's hand and hauled the kid to his feet, both hands still locked in his steel grip. She stayed down, a smart move on her part since she had no way to subdue the boy once she let him up.

"What the hell is going on here?" A man wearing a vest with Jasper's Hardware stitched across the left breast pocket pounded down the wooden walkway and skidded to a halt when he caught sight of the quartet. "Holy shit!" He cupped a hand near his mouth and yelled over his shoulder, "Mabel, call Chief Vance."

Five or six people now stood near, gawking and grumbling, a few with fear in their eyes. Less than a minute passed before Jud heard a siren. *Vance to the rescue. Nothing much has changed around here, I see.* He swung the boy around to face the street as a black and white unit pulled up to the curb, spewing gravel from beneath worn tires.

Now that the law had shown up, the woman stood and let the other boy get up. Jud saw him curl his hands into fists at his side, while light blue eyes narrowed, and his square jaw jutted out. The kid wanted to strike her. Jud shot a warning glance his way, and the kid wiped the aggression off his face.

Chief Vance climbed slowly out of the older model Chevy cruiser, his age probably more an excuse for not hurrying than caution. He casually made his way to the front of the car then stopped, his stance and hand on the gun butt at his waist showing his position of power. His glowering gaze skimmed the crowd, his blue eyes missing nothing.

A chill ran down Jud's spine that not even two tours in Iraq could create. This man was as dangerous today as he had been when Jud was a kid. But when push came to shove, he was a man now, and Vance would not intimidate him.

"Peter. Walter. You two come over here." Vance motioned first the taller boy then the shorter one to his side. Peter, the one Jud still held cuffed with his hands, jerked in his grip. He let the boy go so he could join the police chief. The shorter one called Walter leaped off the curb and stood shoulder to shoulder with Vance. Jud could easily see the resemblance between the two. Square jaw, high forehead, pale hair cut the same, straight nose and those light blue eyes.

Vance jerked a thumb to the shorter boy on his right. "This here is my grandson, Walter." He nodded to the other boy without taking his gaze off Jud. "And this is Peter Dansing, the mayor's son. You remember his daddy." He said that as a statement of fact, not a question.

Yeah, Jud remembered Jack Dansing. A nasty piece of shit when they were kids and probably just as bad now if his son's actions were any example.

Now that he stood alone, Jud knew it was only a matter of time before the crowd recognized and turned on him. As surely as an IED—improvised explosive device—could blow up a troop carrier in a war zone, this commotion had destroyed his hope of slipping into town, taking care of business, then leaving as soon as possible. He had left under harsh circumstances, and memories here in the Smoky Mountains were long. Despite the dense Native American population in these parts, how many Cherokee Indians came through town every day, much less lived there?

"That lady there," Vance pointed to the feisty woman who had helped him stop the fight. "That's the high school counselor, Lottie Amberville. She works with your mother."

Jud turned his upper body toward her and tipped the edge of his tan camo cap. "Ma'am." He put his gaze back on Vance as soon as possible. No telling what the man would come up with as an excuse to get him out of town.

"Miss Amberville, this is…"

"Longtree." She nodded toward his last name stitched over the pocket of his military blouse. One brow arched, her eyes searched his face, seeking information he refused to give her. She tipped her head forward and squinted at him.

Jud waited in silence, his hands down at his side, his face void of expression. If she worked for the school, she knew his mom. If she knew his mom, she probably knew his history. Or at least the public version.

Despite her obvious beauty and the spirit she had demonstrated during the fight, he saw in her eyes the reputation he deliberately left behind twenty years ago. Did she believe the stories about him and the locals? Did she believe the stories about him breaking his mother's heart and threatening the high school principal?

"Jud Longtree." She stepped closer and let her gaze travel down his body then back up to his face.

She wanted to speak out in anger, he could tell by how stiffly she held her body. How hostile her gaze. But rather than spit out her dislike, she clamped her mouth shut with an audible snap.

~ * ~

Lottie watched the men and women standing around them skitter back and start mumbling in stage whispers—'that Indian Jud Longtree'—loud enough for all to hear. She'd lived in Bleaker ten years, and once she met his mother, Mary—the school custodian—she wanted to slap the shit out of a son who could piss off everyone, disregard everything good and leave his mom high and dry without a backward glance. With his record, maybe leaving had been the best thing. But why go so insolently?

He might have been defiant as a youth but not any longer. Now he looked assured and dangerous. Rock solid from his combat cap to his polished military-issued boots, he stood well over six-feet tall. His black hair was shorn to the scalp, his face clean-shaven. Muscled biceps bulged from under his rolled up shirtsleeves, accenting his broad chest and shoulders. Despite his intimidating size, the darkness of his eyes drew her before she yanked her gaze lower, to his luscious full lips.

So what if he was a hunk in full Marine camo? She had no business staring at his lips as if they were candy meant for her pleasure.

Before Chief Vance could say another word, Lottie stepped even closer. Fists tight at her side, she stuck her face nearer his. "Miss Mary seen you yet?"

Longtree nodded once. He turned his dark focus on her, and she drew in a shaky breath. The man epitomized danger. Checking on his mom after all these years didn't make sense. "Why are you here?"

The silence grew heavy. She sensed he wasn't going to answer, even if only to tell her his reasons were none of her business.

5

"That's my question." Vance turned his attention from Lottie back to Jud and began, "Now Longtree, why…" But once again, someone interrupted him.

Into the middle of his questioning came the sound of running feet. Lottie glanced over her shoulder to see Ashley Johnson headed for the crowd. Her best friend was in her usual full-out mode. Just watching the waitress's boundless energy made Lottie tired.

"Lottie! Lottie! What happened? I saw…" The woman stopped so fast she literally rammed into Lottie's shoulder. "I saw you flip that piece of work, Walter Vance, over your shoulder." When she stopped to catch her breath, she finally caught sight of Jud. "Holy shit! Who's he?"

Lottie saw her friend's eyes light up with interest. A smile began that brought out the dimples on each side of Ashley's mouth. Worried that she might become infatuated with a man who wasn't worth the effort, Lottie quickly introduced them. "Ashley Johnson, meet Jud Longtree. Resident bad boy."

She honestly expected a snappy retort from the man, something like *former bad boy*, but Longtree neither said a word nor took his glance off… What was he looking at? She followed his gaze. The clock? Across the street, the town hall clock started chiming. In the booming noise of nine bells, no one moved, but when she turned back to him, someone new had moved onto the crowded sidewalk.

"Jud Longtree?"

Longtree turned to the voice at his left shoulder, blinked once then allowed his face to soften into a grin powerful enough to make Lottie's insides clinch. "Mr. Waverly?" He didn't extend his hand.

Keenan Waverly did though. He eagerly stuck out his thick black hand and grasped Longtree's. "Good to see you, boy." Keenan sucked up his next comment. His eyes twinkled with the brightness of a new morning. "Sorry, Sergeant. I figure you haven't been a boy for quite some time now." Waverly snapped his barrel-shaped body into a tight salute and froze. His expression said he was former military and recognized a superior rank.

Longtree wiped the grin off his face, straightened with a jerk that would have broken a smaller man's spine and swung his hand up into a crisp salute. Both men stood that way for two heartbeats then finished with a snap of hands back to their sides.

Keenan stuck out his hand again, and Longtree took it once more. "Nice to see you home. All those hash marks on your sleeve mean you made Master Sergeant?"

Longtree nodded but remained silent.

Not so Keenan who, like Mary Longtree, worked as a custodian and knew Lottie. "Mary is expecting you. Where is she?" He released Longtree's hand and looked around the marine as if she might be hiding behind him.

"I'm on my way to meet her, sir." Longtree's eyes cut over to Lottie and then Vance, now leaning back against the car's hood, still sandwiched between the two boys. "That is, if there's nothing this lady or the chief needs." The way he said it, one would think him incredibly bored by the fight and following interrogation.

"When did you get to town?" Chief Vance straightened, hitched his gun belt higher and stepped up on to the sidewalk, attempting to take back control of the situation.

"Last night." Longtree never moved a muscle. Lottie wondered if a chunk of granite might move more than this man's face.

While Vance postured for his constituents, Lottie wanted to roll her eyes in exasperation. *Now* he wanted to get official. Other than Longtree helping her break up a fight between two hotheads, she knew of nothing he had done—in the here and now—to warrant such a tone. Picking up where life left off years ago though, was as predictable for Vance's disposition as the morning sun coming up at one end of Main Street and going down at the other.

"Anybody see you come in?" Vance wasn't even taking notes. This maneuvering was the chief's way of delaying Longtree. Lottie had seen this tactic more than once over the years. The man liked to ask questions, even if the answers weren't his business. Vance's reputation was as nasty as Longtree's. The local police chief liked to throw smart-mouths in his jail for an evening then conveniently forget to feed them. Rumor had it he could be even meaner if crossed, but she'd never seen evidence of that.

"My mother, that's all. I got in after nine."

"Why are you in town so early?" Vance advanced a few steps, close enough that he had to strain his neck to see the other man's face. He backed up until he could stand without looking ridiculous.

"Mom went to school. Said she had something to take care of. Said she'd buy me breakfast if I'd meet her at the diner at nine."

Lottie glanced at the clock across the street again and scrunched up her face in disbelief. Fifteen minutes had passed since they had stopped the fight and Vance began his inane questioning. Longtree was late meeting his mother. With all this uproar, why hadn't she shown up already?

Keenan stepped up to the marine's side. "Say, Chief, how about Jud and me walk over to the diner and find Mary? You can find him if you need him."

Lottie could see the chief's reluctance to let Longtree go though he had no reason to hold him.

Just about the time she breathed a sigh of relief, Vance nodded over his shoulder to each of the boys at the car's hood. "What about these two? You got anything to say about them?" Was he daring Longtree to voice a complaint?

"They only bloodied each other." Longtree glanced at Lottie. "You okay, Miss? Did Walter hurt you?"

While his words were impersonal and polite, Lottie saw his expression mellow with concern. She had to wonder if years away from Bleaker and the folks who condemned him had changed him into someone better than the rebel rouser she'd always heard about. After seeing how the chief and townsfolk treated him, Lottie was ready to let the matter drop.

"I'm fine. If this had been on the school campus, these two would serve time in detention hall then do community service." She frowned at Peter and Walter. "I don't know what got into both of you. Best friends. Star athletes. Role models and all. This town's got problems enough without you two mixing it up on a Saturday morning."

She wasn't so ungracious as to ignore Longtree's help. No way could she have broken up that fight alone, and she would have been hurt if she'd tried. "Thanks for your help...breaking up the fight." Her words drifted somewhere toward the middle of his chest. Meeting his eyes was a challenge she wasn't sure she was up to.

"All right then. No charges filed." Vance made shooing noises and waved a hand as if brushing off flies. "Let's move along, folks." People began to step away, probably disappointed that the man did not draw his gun and haul the marine's butt to jail.

And that's what it would have taken to get the man behind bars, Lottie imagined. A gun—a big gun. Intimidation alone wouldn't be enough.

Ashley bumped Lottie's shoulder, drawing her attention away from the men. "Who's that guy, and what got Vance's drawers in a wad?" The woman wasn't subtle when she was curious.

Lottie took her by the arm and turned her back toward the diner further down the block. "I'll tell you over a cup of coffee."

~ * ~

Few if any had gone more than a dozen steps from the center of excitement before a hysterical male scream broke the calm. "Chief! Chief Vance! Help!"

Jud immediately headed for the kid. One quick glance showed the boy wore baseball pants but not the uniform top. His hair lay flat against his skull as if he'd pulled on his t-shirt in a hurry. Pure instinct to correct a wrong made Jud go to him only steps ahead of the school counselor. Chief Vance came a bit slower, his sturdy bulk evidently not used to running.

"What happened?" Jud grabbed the boy's arm to keep him upright. Red in the face from running and panic, his color was fast fading to white. Shock. Before the boy could answer, he bent double and vomited in the gutter. Vance caught up in time to step back as foul-smelling bile spattered, barely missing his boots.

The woman—Lottie—wrapped her arm around the boy's waist. "Take it easy, Lance. Tell us what happened." She pushed the hair off his high forehead and pulled the tail of his t-shirt up to wipe his mouth.

9

Lance gasped, his breath coming shallow and fast. "Mr…Jetter…car out front." He could barely string a sentence together. Jud had seen this kind of terror. "School unlocked." The boy leaned heavily against Lottie. "Wasn't in…office." Lance began to shake, his knees visibly wobbling.

Vance did nothing but watch though Jud could see the kid was about to crash. "Take a seat, kid. Now take a deep breath." His color paled further. "Let's get this off." He pulled the t-shirt over the boy's head and used it to wipe his face, though he was not sweating. A sure sign of shock. "Someone bring a damp cloth and a drink of water." The sound of running feet registered with him. "Hold on. We'll get you cooled off." He passed the wadded shirt to Lottie. "Did you find Mr. Jetter?"

"Yeah." Pant, pant. "Needed uniform. Gym." What little color Lance had regained washed out of his face once more, and his eyes began to glaze.

Given signs the boy was about to pass out, Jud patted his face to keep his attention focused and gratefully accepted a wet dishtowel Ashley handed him. "Come on, Lance. Stay with me."

By now, Vance had taken a knee in front of the trio. He offered no help but demanded answers. "So what happened, kid?"

For once, Jud agreed with the police chief's impatience. Where was his mom? "Anyone seen Mary Longtree? She in the diner?"

"She wasn't there just now," Ashley said from behind him.

"Shit, Mom's probably still at school." He'd have been over there in a shot if the need for intel hadn't come first. *Always protect yourself. Always be prepared.* He shook Lance hard to keep him conscious.

"Hey, take it easy!" Lottie protested as she attempted to shove his hands away.

"Zip it, lady. We need to know what's going on before we rush in there." His glare sent her back to the boy's other side without protest.

"Come on, kid, before you crater on us again. What happened?" Vance all but yelled.

For once, he and Vance agreed.

"Gym lights off. Reflection on floor." Lance's eyes grew wide, and his chin began to tremble. His mouth must have gone dry because he licked his lips and swallowed a few times. Unexpected tears welled in his eyes and slipped over to make shiny tracks down brown cheeks. "Mr... head... blood..." He swallowed again, his eyes focused inward on what he'd seen.

The tension in those around Jud was more than he could bear. The feeling of knowing a bomb was about to go off but not knowing how or why screwed him tighter than a drumhead. He shook the kid impatiently. "Did you see anyone else, damn it?" Was his mom hurt?

"Head bashed in... Blood..."

Not waiting to hear what else the boy might say, Jud took off running.

"Ashley, stay with Lance!" Lottie caught up to him though he was in a flat-out run. All he heard was his breathing and that of the counselor, along with the noise of a car starting up and coming down the street.

Jud gave Vance credit for speed when necessary. The surly chief pulled the cruiser up to the school at the same time he got there.

"Wait a minute, Longtree." Chief Vance yelled at Jud as he jerked the front door open. "You can't just barge into a possible crime scene."

As much as he wanted to get to Jetter and find his mom, he knew Vance was right. He waited while the man jogged up to him.

"If someone in there is hurt then we need an ambulance." Vance turned to see who among the town's people had followed. Most had. Spotting the man from the hardware store, he yelled, "Jasper, call 9-1-1 and tell Dispatch to send Clyde, Danny and Ernest to the school. Send an ambulance, too." Vance shoved Jud aside and pulled his gun. "The rest of you stay out here."

Lottie pushed past Jud into the dim hall. "I'm staying."

Vance nodded but said nothing else. Jud had a feeling that the chief might have butted heads with the woman before and come up on the short end of the stick. Besides, arguing would waste time.

"I'm going, too. Mom's in there somewhere." Jud nodded toward the hallway. "Let's check out Jetter first."

Vance sputtered, "Why the hell should you come!"

"I'm trained military," Jud replied, summarily dismissing the man's indignation. "This arguing is taking up time. Let's go." He set off down the hall, moving close to the wall, toward the closed double doors of the gym.

Behind him, Vance growled, "Son of a bitch!" Footsteps moved up quickly, and Jud let the chief take the lead, a sense of urgency making a pissing contest for leadership unimportant.

Vance motioned Jud and Lottie to one side as he eased one door open and slipped in. He scanned the area then nodded to Jud who entered, Lottie on his heels. Like a trio of ghosts, they moved in single-minded unison along the wall toward the bleachers.

A sick feeling settled in Jud's stomach when he saw the body. He swallowed once. Mathew Jetter, the school's principal, lay sprawled on his right side facing them, his back pressed hard against the bottom bleacher, his eyes still open, his left arm twisted awkwardly at his side. Blood pooled under his head and smeared the edge of the wooden step.

Mathew dead? How? Why? This man stepped in as a father, saved Jud's life in a way. And now he lay here dead? Jud's throat tightened. He wanted to throw up. Mathew gone? His rock, besides his… Suddenly he realized someone was missing—his mother. "Mom?" he said softly, desperately, his eyes shifting the scan the gym.

Vance holstered his gun and went down on one knee. A hand to the throat and he shook his head. Even to the untrained eye, it was obvious the man was dead.

"Lottie, can we get some lights turned on in here?"

"Yeah." She swallowed hard enough that Jud heard. "I have to get the master key." Dazed, her face was pale in the faint glow from the windows. She focused on the body at her feet. One hand to her mouth, she ran off toward the office area.

Vance heaved his thick body off the floor with a sigh. Almost as pale as the boy that had sent them there, he swallowed as if keeping bile down. Sweat beaded his forehead above a face drawn with grief. "A damn fine man. Hell of an accident. An accident…until I can investigate," he repeated in a dull voice as he pressed his fingers against watery eyes.

Jud wasn't listening to the chief bemoan the death of a good man. Where was his mother? "Vance, I'm going to look around. Mom's not at the diner where we were going to meet. She has to be here. This could be an accident. Then again, maybe not. If not, the killer might still be here."

"You can't go off on your own, boy." Vance no sooner got that out of his mouth than both heard heavy footsteps coming down the hall.

"Chief?"

"In here, Clyde. Wait there."

Three uniformed officers stopped at the door. Following proper crime scene procedures, they would not enter until told to do so. The overhead lights began to warm up with a dim glow. In a minute or two, they would be at full capacity. In the meantime, the men could see around the gym well enough.

"Clyde, you stay with Jetter. Radio Dispatch and have them send the ME. Ernest, take a look around the rest of the school. Don't take any chances in case someone's here that shouldn't be. Then hot foot it to my cruiser and get the crime scene kit. Tape off every entrance to the school so folks don't wander in. Danny, haul Lottie Amberville outta here. Round up that kid, Lance, who reported this. Keep Amberville and the kid to one side, but separated. Then work crowd control. This is a crime scene, and civilians aren't welcomed."

Clyde pulled out his radio and began a soft-voiced conversation with his dispatcher. Ernest drew his gun and left to search the school. As small as the building was, it would take them longer to search the gym area as it would take the officer to check the other rooms. Danny headed to the office, with the thankless task of removing the school counselor and keeping the curious out. Jud suspected getting Lottie Amberville out of the building might take a lot longer than searching the place.

He wished he had the equipment he used in Iraq. A heat-seeking device to locate bodies. His gun. A knife. Lacking equipment though, he was still a trained killer.

"Okay, hot shot. Let's go. You can put that fancy training to use." Vance once again took out his gun, Jud on his heels. Empowered by the gun in his hand, Vance moved forward quietly on the balls on his feet, the gun held confidently in a two-handed grip. His head swiveled back and forth.

At the equipment room, Jud checked the doorknob. Locked.

They moved further along the gray cinderblock wall toward the doors leading to the dressing rooms. Bleaker High had only one gym but separate dressing areas complete with showers. They ducked into the boys' dressing room. With the air conditioning off, they entered an eerie silence. Vance's breathing sounded winded, a bit stressed. Jud still breathed slow and easy.

A memory of Fallujah in Iraq returned to him. The pressure that ate at a man's nerves, stole his confidence. His squad had participated in this kind of scenario: the house-to-house search, tension so high that the stress was visible in each face. *Prepare to kill or capture the enemy, be cautious of wounding innocents. Prepare for a trap, be wary of each turn.*

Vance waved him down a row of lockers. Glad to do something besides follow a small town police chief, he peeled off and began his own reconnaissance. They met at the end of the room and took up positions on either side of the shower room door. Nothing blocked their view of showerheads and benches. No one in there.

More and more worried that something was wrong or his mother would have showed up by now, Jud led the way out of the dressing room. Vance put a hand on his arm and pulled him back. Following went against his instincts and training, but in this case, who led was not as important as finding his mom.

Only one area left to search. With no word back from Ernest, they could only assume Mary was in the girls' dressing room if she was still in the building at all. Vance again motioned him to check lockers. When they met at the final door, Jud saw a curtain separated each shower. They had to search each stall individually. If a perpetrator hid in one, they were pushing him to the wall.

Vance pulled one arm back, wiped the sweat off his upper lip and pressed a sleeve to his damp forehead. Could be heat in the un-air conditioned building, Jud thought, or the nerves of someone not used to a manhunt.

The chill of a search that could end in death settled over him. Why he wasn't sure. Gut instincts and twenty years in the Marines maybe.

His grip once more secure on his gun, Vance stepped forward. As if they were a military unit, Jud jerked each curtain back while the chief trained his weapon into the stall.

One shower stall left. Jud's stomach cramped. He licked his lips as he nodded to Vance. A flick of his wrist and the curtain pulled back to disclose…

"Mom!" Jud fell on his knees, his finger frantically searching for a pulse. When the slow ragged thread grazed his fingers, he almost cried. "Call 9-1-1!" Desperately wanting to pick up his mother and cradle her against him, he knew if he moved her, he might hurt her more. Mary lay crumpled on the ceramic floor, brown liquid splashed on the wall and splattered on her clothes. An empty cup—her morning coffee—lay on its side in the corner. Like Jetter, blood pooled under her head. But not as much. She was still alive. Jud could be satisfied with that.

When she regained consciousness, she'd tell him what happened. Did she come back here to hide? Did someone hit her? If someone followed her, why was she still alive? Too many questions and no answers.

In the distance, he heard Vance directing EMTs to the dressing room. They could do Mathew Jetter no good, but his mom was a different matter.

"Miss Mary?" One of the EMTs peered into the stall. "Sorry, sir. You'll have to step aside."

Jud quickly moved out of the way, as two men rolled a gurney into the shower room. The stringent odor of disinfectant mingled with the still-fragrant coffee spill to set his nerves throbbing. His fist crumpled the shower curtain into a tight knot. The compact space magnified every sound, making him jump when one of the EMTs spoke.

"I'm Gary." The man next to his mom nodded toward the other man. "That's my partner, Lew." Gary snapped on latex gloves then pulled out a monitor and stethoscope.

The only family Jud had left lay on the floor, bleeding. The thought of losing her to some maniac like he'd lost his father tore at his guts. All he could see was the here and now. If Mary Longtree died, he would never forgive himself. Any good he might have done in the later part of his life wouldn't make up for the pain he had caused her when he'd lived in Bleaker. "She okay?"

"Her pulse is thread, and she's lost a lot of blood." Gary told him what he already knew. "Looks like she either hit her head when she fell or was knocked down." The EMT pressed a gauze pad to his mother's forehead and taped it. Wedging into the tight space, they carefully secured a cervical collar around her neck and laid a backboard next to her. "On my mark," Gary told his partner. "One, two, three." They rolled her on her back, onto the board. Gary covered her and laid the monitor between her legs. They lifted her to the gurney and strapped her in.

Maneuvering with care, they pushed the gurney out of the tiny area and into the gym. The rolling rubber wheels sounded weird in the open space. A rhythmic squishing sort of sound. Both men ignored Vance and the deputy who stood by the body. The needs of the living came before those of the dead.

Jud walked beside Mary. His skin cold. His eyes dry.

"Where you going, Longtree?" Vance's question boomed off the gym walls. Because of the resonance, his voice sounded menacing.

"I'll be with my mother at the hospital if you need me." Jud let his words trail back from the hallway. He didn't bother looking at the officers. Focused on his mom, he tried to ignore the crowd gathered outside the front door. The sun now lay obscured behind a thickening veil of clouds, the morning's warmth having fled into an uncomfortable stillness. Lottie Amberville, a hand over her mouth as if she were going to be sick, watched them pass with Mary Longtree's pale copper-colored face and stark black hair harsh against the white gurney sheets. Tears glistened on her cheeks. For whom or why Jud wasn't certain nor did he care.

~ * ~

Vance had just gotten the crime scene bag from Ernest when

Henry Scott showed up. Bleaker's only family practice doctor, Henry also served as the county medical examiner.

"Have you finished your investigation yet?" Henry held his bag rather than lay it down and stayed at the door instead of entering, to avoid contaminating the scene.

"Just started." Vance opened a large duffel bag and took out a Nikon digital camera. *This is gonna be a long day.* He grimaced. Handing the camera to Ernest, he moved to the middle of the gym. "I want a panoramic from here so we can see how the body is positioned in relation to the door and bleachers. When you're finished, move in for more detailed shots while I do the sketches and take notes."

"You act like this is a murder instead of an accident." Henry craned his neck in order to follow Vance's steps back to the body.

"Probably not. With so little to do around Bleaker," he confided, "we study police procedures just to kill time. Might as well use 'em now." Vance nodded to the body. "Looks like Mathew slipped somehow and hit his head on the riser. But we found Mary Longtree injured under unexplained circumstances, so…" He pulled out a pad and started taking notes, his suspicions left unspoken. "You can come over here, Doc. But…"

"Yeah, I know. Don't touch anything." Henry moved to Vance's side and gave a low whistle. "Lots of blood. I don't know…"

"I'm not taking any chances. If this is something other than an accident and I let the investigation slide, I'll have my butt in a sling, and this office will be closed." He moved aside so Ernest could take close-up photos of the head and body.

While his deputy snapped one shot after another, Vance verbally reviewed the steps of a crime scene investigation that he and the other members of his police force often studied. "Who? Mathew Jetter— principal of Bleaker High School. Incident reported by student Lance Bolls. Motivation? Unknown at this time." Vance jerked his head toward the body. "Doc, take a look without touching at this point, and tell me if you see anything that ought not to be there or anything that should but is missing."

Henry squatted and twisted first one way then another to get a better look. "He's wearing jeans and a polo shirt. Typical for what I've seen him wear on weekends. Still has his watch and there's a bulge in his hip pocket—from what little I can see of his back. Looks like his wallet is still there."

Vance continued his inventory of questions that needed answering. "What happened? Humm, Jetter came to school on a Saturday morning. Nothing unusual for him though I don't know the specific reason he came today. Mary Longtree came here as well. Which *is* unusual. She only does custodial duties during the week. Keenan Waverly works custodial for weekend events." Vance squatted beside Henry though he let out a sigh when he did so. His age was beginning to tell on his knees. "When did this happen? Not long ago from the looks of that blood and his eyes, I'd guess."

Henry bent lower. "Agreed. The eyeballs are filmed but not cloudy yet. I'd say less than two hours, certainly no more than that. Closer to one hour, I'm thinking. I'll know more when I can move him. Blood is coagulated but not dried."

"Scene secured at…" Vance checked his watch. "Nine-fifty a.m. on Saturday April twenty-eighth. First officer on scene—Police Chief Theo Vance. Officers following—Clyde Bell, Danny Threen and Ernest Lee. Others on scene when the body was discovered—Jud Longtree, former resident—with a history, I'm gonna add, and Lottie Amberville, school counselor." He put a hand to the floor and pushed his body upright, suppressing a groan as he stood. "Ernest, stand down for a minute until I finish checking things. Then we'll move the body, and you can take pictures from that angle."

Ernest waited not far behind Vance as Henry stood. "If this wasn't an accident then could it be…" Henry didn't look so well.

"Murder? Won't know until we gather all the evidence and you do the autopsy and establish cause and TOD. Time of death will be important." Vance turned his back to the body, Mathew Jetter—a man he'd known for thirty years. He seldom counted his friends. He had few, but this man had been one—one who supported and cared.

Shaking off his feelings, he continued his oral investigation list. "We have to find points of entry and exits though I suspect anyone could have walked into the office area, like that kid did." Vance clicked the end of his ballpoint pen several times. "Eyewitnesses? Humm, unknown except possibly Mary Longtree. And she's unconscious."

"What happened to Mary?" Henry blinked in surprise.

"You must have missed the ambulance that pulled out. Longtree and I found her unconscious in the girls' shower room. Head wound but can't tell if she fell or someone pushed her. As soon as she wakes up, I'll have more answers."

Vance pulled a police sketchpad and a tape measure from the bag. "Doc, I'm gonna do these sketches. You gather blood samples, and Clyde can take them to the lab in Spartanburg."

For the next thirty minutes, with Ernest's help, he made three sketches showing the body's position from various angles in reference to objects in the gym, like the doors and bleacher.

"Okay, Doc, you can have a look now." Vance waved Ernest to one side, the camera ready to record the doctor's findings.

Henry set his medical bag at his feet, pulled out latex gloves and slipped them on. He also put on a knee-length disposable lab coat. With flashlight and thermometer in hand, he approached the body.

"Primary wound seems to be blunt force trauma to the head, possibly caused by a fall against the bleacher. Blood is congealed but not dried. Splatters are consistent with this sort of injury. Elongated when he fell. There's blood on his face as if he lay in it as he bled out, but then it smeared as if he turned. Considerably more on his right cheek where he laid in it."

Henry touched the left shoulder, the one upper-most since the body had landed on the right side with the back jammed tightly against the first row of bleacher. "Ernest, get pictures of this. If there is one thing unusual so far, it's the position of this left arm. Rather than falling forward on to the floor, his arm is twisted back as if he was reaching for the bleacher to help him stand. I suspect he did not die immediately." He reached out and pulled the polo shirt away from the body at the belt line. "Now that's odd."

"What's the matter?" Vance bent down, his hands propped on each knee, the leather of his belt and holster making a grainy rubbing sound.

"There's blood pooled beneath his ribcage, on the right side. Not much, but that's not consistent with the head wound." One knee down, Henry put a hand on the shoulder and one on the hip and forced the body forward, away from the wood where it has been jammed.

"Holy shit!" Ernest said what Vance and the doc had to be thinking.

For the first time, they saw a knife sticking out of the lower right side of Jetter's back, hidden between the body and bleacher.

"Damn! Murder after all!" Vance swore at the evidence that showed his friend didn't die accidently.

"Chief, I can't say yet whether this knife killed Mathew or he died of a head wound," Henry protested, as he knelt by the body, the knife still in shadows.

Engrossed in this latest discovery, Vance ignored the medical examiner. "This changes everything. I need to get some Luminol and check for blood in this gym. Mathew's death might have been suspicious before, but this puts a lid on it. Evidence and witnesses are even more critical." He snapped out orders like a drill sergeant. "Henry, get blood samples from under the body and that pooling. Check that handle for blood. When you're finished, we'll dust it for fingerprints. Ernest, get up on that bleacher and get some detailed shots. The light's not too good with his back still so close to that first riser, but do the best you can. Damn! Murder," he repeated in a strangled voice.

"We've never had a murder in Bleaker." Henry bent over the body, the thermometer in his gloved hands positioned to take a liver temperature reading.

"Yes, we have." Vance spoke matter-of-factly, as if this were an ordinary dinner conversation while he viciously snapped the sketchpad closed and folded the tape measure with over-stated care.

"Since when?"

"Years ago. Before you came."

"Well, I never heard about it," Henry commented over his shoulder as he unfolded a body bag.

Vance knelt and leaned in to get a closer look at the knife. *Is there writing on the handle?* "Hey, Ernest, get that flash down here closer, and take some pictures of that handle for me. Several angles."

"Chief?" Clyde stepped through the doorway.

"Yeah?" Vance watched his deputy stoop and twist in order to get decent shots at impossible angles behind the body.

"Crowd outside is pretty upset. Anything you want to tell them?"

"Humm, just a minute."

Ernest stood and pushed a few buttons on the camera in order to preview the shots he had just taken. His face paled even under high intensity lights. "Uh, Chief?"

"Yeah, what'd you get?" He took the camera and pressed the arrow key, scrutinizing each shot of the knife. By fractions, his lips drew up until he grinned like a fool or someone who'd just won the lottery. "Got ja, you damn red skin."

In the last shot taken, a name stood out plainly, carved into the bone handle of a hand-made knife. A name accented by smeared blood. One name.

J Longtree.

Chapter Two

Jud sat in the waiting area, his total attention on the door across the room. The tiny hospital seemed to have everything Dr. Hooker needed to treat his mom. At least that's what the doctor said as they wheeled her through ER and out of sight.

"We'll do scans and begin an IV for blood to replace what she's lost then maybe surgery. Can't tell yet, Sergeant. But I'll keep you informed."

Within ten minutes, a nurse brought forms for him to sign, admitting Mary and giving permission for surgery if necessary.

Ten minutes after that, the same nurse directed him to a consultation room where Dr. Hooker waited. "Mrs. Longtree has a concussion and bleeding in the brain. I have to be honest. She's in bad shape. Very bad shape. We have to do surgery to relieve the pressure. Dr. Latner will do the procedure. He's on his way. Then we'll put her in a medically induced coma to avoid stress. Within twenty-four to forty-eight hours, we should be able to start bringing her out of that. Then we wait to see how she does." He shook Jud's hand, and his eyes were sympathetic. "We'll do our best, son."

"Thank you, sir." Just like when he was a kid and the world crowded in on him, Jud sank deep into himself. His mom believed in the prayers of their Cherokee ancestors. He believed in nothing but what he could experience. For a split second, he regretted not spending more time with her the night before. She'd been willing to sit up all night and visit, but she'd also said she needed to be at school at eight.

22

They arranged to meet for breakfast and went to bed.

But he arose long before dawn to visit his father. Chants from his childhood learned at his father's side came easily in the dark. A small fire took away the dawn's chill and soothed his loneliness.

Would he soon visit the graves of both parents and sing to the ancestors for their spirit trip?

In his mind, he sought the help that his mother had taught him to ask for as a youngster. "Great Spirit, I ask you to see my mother, Mary Longtree, and heal her body." Could he ask that same Spirit to have pity on her? On him? He settled back in the cushioned chair and stilled, focusing his energy into the closest thing he could come to that resembled prayer. "Ancestors of the mighty Cherokee, *my* ancestors, I am Jud, son of Mary and Jacob. I ask for your wisdom." He did not know how to say what he wanted. His mother back, healthy and strong, yes. But more than that. What if...? The words came to him in a more modern form but the ancestors would forgive and probably understand. "I ask the ancestors for peace. Help me accept this. Guide me through this time. If my mother comes through, I thank you. If Mom..." Jud had a hard time getting the word past his lips, "dies, help me to be strong and accept what has happened and cannot be changed. And," he paused, uncertain if his forefathers would assist in this request, "help me find out what happened to her and my friend, Mathew Jetter. He wasn't Cherokee, but he was a good man."

His mind at peace finally, his skin began to prickle as if a thousand eyes watched him. Used to leading men into war but not being the object of someone's attention in peace, he eased one eye open and looked around. Damn!

Lottie Amberville sat next to him, watching him like a hawk. From the way she wiggled, she wanted to say something but respected his closed eyes. She looked like a live electric wire, buzzing with energy. If he closed his eye, maybe she'd leave. No such luck. Some sixth sense must have told her he was aware of her presence.

"Sergeant Longtree, how is Mary?" She grabbed his arm as she spoke and scooted so close that her leg lay against his. Too late, she realized how intimate they were and moved away a few inches, but she still held his arm. The more worried she was the tighter she held on. If he didn't ease her off, he'd wear her fingerprints on his skin for a week.

"She's in surgery. The doctor said she's hurt pretty bad. But he's hopeful." Having answered her question, he tried to ignore her, but it seemed Lottie Amberville was not the ignoring type. That long black hair he had admired on the sidewalk fell in waves over her shoulder and lay just above her breasts. Her skin was a warm latte color, and her eyes were dark brown. Smooth narrow brows accented her large eyes and complimented her nose with its broad tip above a mouth that stretched wide, framed by narrow blush-colored lips.

Tall and tanned. When she smiled, like she did at his news, her face lit up, white teeth flashing and eyes glowing. Despite the seriousness of his mom's condition, he couldn't ignore Lottie's attraction. If she didn't dislike him so much, he might have taken her to the diner for coffee and some interesting conversation before sampling a little hot se…

Jud's thoughts halted right there. He'd had women in the past but never one from Bleaker, and he wasn't about to go there now. Disgusted with himself, he pulled his cap low over his eyes, crossed his arms over his chest—definitely closing himself off from her—and slumped further in the chair. If he had to, he'd close his eyes and start snoring just to get rid of her. Time passed without a word between them. He wondered how long she'd stay. He didn't realize how perceptive she was or how short her temper was.

"You're such a jerk. If you want me to leave, just say so. No need to pretend you're asleep." She spoke succinctly, her words bitten off, heavy with anger that rang in her tone, deepened her voice. "I didn't realize Marines could be such cowards." Though she sensed he wanted her gone, she had yet to stand.

His patience at an end, wanting her gone, wondering why she was bugging him to begin with, he finally slid his eyes open and gave her a resigned look, his face once more devoid of any emotions, much like it was when he dealt with his men. This situation had only one practical solution, he quickly decided.

"You are wrong about two things. Marines are not cowards, Miss

Amberville. Nor am I a jerk. But you are right about one."

Her eyes opened even wider at his blunt speech. "And what would that be?" She sat with her hands on her hips, a rather ludicrous pose, he thought.

"I do want you to leave." He gave her the level deadeye stare that he used on new recruits to his squad. No way could she doubt his sincerity.

Like a vacuum cleaner, he saw her suck up air, then turn red. Fury washed over her face; her lips narrowed while her eyes squinted.

"Damn, I so do not see how you can be related to Miss Mary!" She snapped to her feet like someone had pulled a string up her spine. Her body radiated suppressed energy, as evidenced by her loud comment. "I hope you leave before Mary discovers what a jackass you are!" Several people in the room turned at her words, and Jud wanted to disappear. He hated people like her, those who lived on the edge of emotions all the time.

"Go home, Miss Amberville. Better yet, go take care of those kids who need a soft shoulder to cry on." His effort to distract her seemed to work. For a moment, she appeared furious with him, then like a switch turned off, she refocused her attention on those in need of help to get past the high school principal's death.

Her hair sent flying over her shoulders by a magnificent toss of her head, the woman stomped out of the room but attempted to have the last word, so to speak, when she slammed the door hard enough to rattle several pictures on the wall.

Once more, Jud ignored those around him and focused on his problems: women problems, first his mom and now that hot-headed beauty that both aggravated the hell out him and called to his body at the same time.

~ * ~

"Longtree!" The police chief bounced the waiting room door opened as hard as Lottie had shut it.

"What do you want?" Jud sat forward, elbows on knees, hands clasped together between. He wasn't in the mood to put up with any

25

hassles.

"Stand up." Vance came into the room, flanked by the officers Jud had seen earlier at the gym.

He didn't want to give the chief any reason to mess with him so he stood. "I'm not bothering anyone. I'm just waiting here to see how Mom is."

"Turn around." Vance advanced to within six feet and pulled out a pair of handcuffs.

"What the hell are you planning on doing with those?" Jud widened his stance as his hands curled into tight fists. His pulse pounded; Vance wouldn't be making a play like this unless he thought he had something.

"I'm gonna cuff you, read you your rights, then haul you off to jail." No matter that Vance talked big, he stayed where he was, the cuffs held loosely in his hand.

"On what charges?" Though Jud spoke quietly, no one could doubt the menace in his tone. All his focus subtly changed from his mother's situation to his own.

"The murder of Mathew Jetter." The chief barely managed to contain a smile.

"What!" Jud took a step forward. "He was my friend. My best friend! I didn't kill Mathew!" He could tell the chief was delighted to have a suspect and even more thrilled that he was the one.

"I have evidence that said you did. You going to cooperate, or do we have to take you down?"

Vance wanted him to fight.

Years of hard work, keeping his nose clean, making a better life just went down the toilet. Jud was innocent but would have to prove it in order to get away from the police chief. Besides he came here for a good reason; his mother didn't need this shit when she regained consciousness. The pride every Marine takes in controlling himself in a bad situation tempered a deep desire to beat the crap out of Theo Vance.

He turned his back to the men. "I'm not giving you the satisfaction of hitting me. I'll go, but I did *not* kill Mathew Jetter. There is no motive…" Jud winced as first one cuff then the other snapped tightly around his wrists. "No reason to kill him. If not for Mathew, I'd be in jail or dead by now."

"Well, I'm taking you to jail and if that evidence holds up, you might just wind up dead." Vance jerked Jud hard to one side, knocking him off balance. He had to scramble to regain his balance and that pissed him off. But he refused to fight the local law.

As Vance and his henchmen shoved him through the doorway, his mind finally began to focus on something other than the chief's nasty attitude. "Just what evidence do you have against me?"

Vance didn't answer. He crushed Jud's cap on the pretense of protecting his head as he put him in the back of the cruiser.

"What evidence, damn it!"

Before Vance closed the back door, he leaned forward and whispered, "Something you can't argue with."

"I didn't kill him! I didn't!" But Vance slamming the door cut off Jud's choleric bellow.

~ * ~

Lottie spent the next three hours in the town's library, consoling students and faculty. Jetter was a widower with no family; his students were his children, his staff his family. While he was firm with all, most considered him a fair man.

"I'll be here tomorrow after church if you need to talk, Sharon." Lottie hugged a tearful senior before sending her home with her parents.

"I'll reserve the reading room for you tomorrow, Lottie." Mabel Turner, the librarian, made a note on her calendar. "I still have a hard time believing Mathew is gone." She took her glasses off and used a Kleenex to wipe away her tears. "Do you think the school will be open Monday?"

"I honestly don't know. I'll ask Chief Vance if he's through investigating the accident." Lottie smoothed her blouse and pushed thick hair off her forehead. She'd been in Spartanburg attending a counseling conference Friday and had driven home early that Saturday morning. She still had on the clothes she had worn to the last workshop session. "I'm going to stop by the diner and get a take-out sandwich and coffee and go home. I got up early this morning. Then…" She let out a sigh that was long and deep. "I'll stop by the police station and talk to Vance. The kids and staff need to go on as best they can with Mathew dead and Miss Mary unconscious in the hospital." She waved to Mabel and eased out of the library. No sooner did she step out from under the awning and off the curb than a burst of cold rain caught her by surprise. "Damn, when did the weather change? Just what we need today of all days," she muttered as she made a dash for the diner where Ashley waited tables.

Lottie refrained from shaking her head and sending splatters of rain all over the entryway to the Blue Ridge Diner. The place was practically deserted for the middle of a Saturday afternoon. She only saw a few heads in booths. Folks usually had pie and coffee at the diner after making their weekly trips to the grocery and hardware stores. "Hey, Ashley. Not much happening today, huh."

"Lottie! Did you hear?" Ashley practically jumped Lottie when she tried to sit at the counter.

"Hear what?"

"Vance arrested that Longtree fellow for Mathew's murder!" Ashley held a towel in her hand so tightly her skin was white.

"Murder?" Lottie had to sit. She suddenly felt faint. And a bit sick. So Mathew's death was no accident. "Who told you?"

"Clay Benner was walking up the block and saw Vance's cruiser pull in behind the police station. He heard the chief giving that man his rights and Longtree denying that he had anything to do with Mathew's murder. Because the time of death was so recent—less than an hour before they found him—Vance said the guy killed Mathew then circled around the block and started to walk to the diner innocent as you please. Clay ran over here and practically shouted the news to the late breakfast bunch." A normally happy person with a ready smile, just then Ashley looked like she wanted to cry. "I knew that fellow was bad news when you were so short with him this morning."

Lottie shivered. Was it the chill of air conditioning against her wet skin and clothes that made her shake or something worse? Some premonition that things were about to change in Bleaker. And then the implications of Vance hauling Jud Longtree to jail hit her. *He didn't do it.* Her mental thought found voice. "He didn't do it. And I can prove it," Lottie said in an excited yell.

"What!" Ashley hollered then lowered her voice and grabbed Lottie by the arm hard enough that the pain got her attention. "What do you mean, he didn't do it? You *know* Vance. He wouldn't do shit like that if he didn't think he could get away with it."

"But Longtree didn't kill Mathew if he'd only been dead an hour or less. Heck, even three hours. I *know*!" Before Lottie could explain further, a couple approached the register.

"Stay right here, girlfriend. I'm the only one on duty right now so I have to ring up the bill for Mayor Dansing and his wife, but you have to explain what you just said." Ashley gave Lottie a hard glare and reluctantly went to the end of the counter. "Good afternoon." She scanned the receipt. "That'll be ten-seventy two. How was that chocolate pie?"

"Delicious as usual, Ashley." Jack Dansing seemed distracted. He didn't stop to chat like Lottie had seen him do in times past. Beside him, his wife Julie, a pleasant enough woman, the epitome of a small town mayor's wife, said nothing, intent apparently on leaving between rain showers. Unfortunately, she'd have to get wet or wait; rain began hitting the large window just as the mayor took his change. Rather than leave, they stood by the door while Ashley returned to Lottie.

"Now what's this about you can prove Longtree's not guilty?" She talked in a low tone, her face furrowed with concern, her gaze shifting from side to side. "Vance is gonna have a fit," she hissed.

"Yeah, he will, but I spotted Jud Longtree and stayed to watch him for at *least* three hours then followed him into town. He never had time to go to the school, kill Mathew then meet me on the sidewalk to bust up that fight." Lottie gasped softly at an unsavory thought. "That means the killer's still free. I have to tell Vance." She jumped off the stool, but Ashley held her back again.

"You can't go over there looking the way you do! Vance will

laugh you out of the station. You know what a chauvinist he is. Go home, take a quick shower then see him. You need all the credibility you can get with that man. And right now, you look like a drowned rat. Besides, I have a feeling sitting in jail a few hours won't kill Longtree." By now, Ashley seemed ambivalent about Mary Longtree's son.

Lottie felt the same way. At first, she only saw the man who hurt Mary by staying away. With good cause. The man must have driven Mathew crazy when he got to high school. By the end of her first year at Bleaker High as counselor, she had heard tales of pranks and antics perpetrated by Jud.

She'd once approached Mathew and asked him about the kid. "Mathew, tell me about Jud Longtree. Everyone said he was bad and should've been in jail."

"Don't believe everything you hear, Lottie. There's always more to the stories than you know. What happens in public is often a different story in private." That's all he would say. While his words dismissed her inquiry, his body language bespoke sadness. Did Mathew consider himself a failure, the reason for Jud leaving town? That was the only conversation she and Mathew ever had about the man, though she heard about 'that red boy' whenever someone recalled 'the old days'.

Lottie ran a hand through her damp hair, then smoothed her wrinkled slacks. "You're right. He won't wilt sitting there for a few more minutes. I was going to get something to eat, but I'll do that after I talk to Vance. I'm going home, but I'll talk to you later."

The mayor and his wife had left sometime during their conversation so Lottie pushed the door opened to see that rain fell steadily now. "Damn. And my car's still got a flat on the other side of the cemetery."

~ * ~

Warm and dry after a hasty shower, Lottie left the bathroom, with a towel thrown over her head, vigorously wringing water out of her long hair. The house's utter stillness didn't bother her; she had no roommate or significant other. Not even a pet.

Her back to the hallway door, she pulled the towel off just in time to hear heavy breathing. An arm came around her neck from behind! Cutting off her air! Hot muscles squeezed her throat while holding her in a rock hard grasp. She automatically grabbed the dark-clad arm strangling her with both of her hands. She clawed for another deep lung of air, but found nothing. Grunts and growls came from behind her, as if someone were putting out a lot of energy to kill her.

A twist to the left did not release the arm but did throw the person off balance. A lamp on the dresser fell against the wall and shattered on the hard wood floor. For that, Lottie got a kick in the back of the calf. The arm hitched higher under her chin, and the pressure resumed.

She gagged, tried to cough but had no air to do so. She tried to dip her chin and bite the flesh so tantalizingly close to her mouth, but she couldn't gain any advantage. Switching tactics, she dropped an arm, swung it forward then drove it back as hard as she could. For a moment, she thought she was free; the person behind her grunted in pain, an odd sounding whimper. Her assault on the man earned her more pain. He swung her around and slammed her head into the wall. Lottie had lifted her legs, hoping to throw the man off balance, but when he bashed her head into the wall the second time, her legs went limp, and her grip weakened on the forearm that was choking her.

Her sight faded in and out, gray to blurred colors outside the window. A great roaring began in her ears though a mechanical buzzing intervened now and then. Added to that cacophony of sounds came a thudding. Lottie knew it was her heart in its final moments, struggling to beat without oxygen. She was going to die and didn't know why.

As suddenly as the attack began, it ended. The assailant threw her toward the wall where she bounced once and sank to the floor. A rag doll by now, Lottie was just this side of unconsciousness. The back door at the end of the hallway rattled, but then she might have imagined that. Louder heavier footsteps pounded down the hall toward her bedroom.

"Miss Lottie? Good God, woman, what happened!" Keenan Waverly stood in her doorway for maybe a heartbeat before he ran to her. All she could do was draw in deep draughts of air and try to keep

31

the shaking under control. To breathe felt like heaven; shaking felt like hell.

"Someone…" Her throat was too raw to speak above the merest whisper. So she pointed to the door and motioned around the left. One hand covered the bruised skin on her throat while the other held her propped off the floor. Her bathrobe covered her, but Lottie wondered if she would ever again remember what real warmth felt like.

The school custodian ran out of the bedroom, and for a few minutes, Lottie heard him at the back door. Finally, she heard the door shut, the lock click into place and footsteps approaching.

"Whoever it was is gone now." Keenan entered the bedroom and knelt by her. "We have to get you to the hospital, ma'am. I'm calling 9-1-1." He pulled out his cell phone and punched the three numbers. Though she tried to protest, Keenan wasn't listening. He helped her stand, and together they sat on the end of the bed. "I'm thinking I need to call the police as well."

By now, Lottie could care less who came. Her whole body throbbed, the point of her shoulder where it hit the wall, her knees where she fell at some point—pulsated with each beat of her heart. The knot on her temple ached so badly the pain almost blocked out everything else. But not quite.

The ambulance must have been at the hospital, five blocks away, because she heard it coming almost immediately. Another siren joined the first one, and all too soon, that noise added to the jackhammers going off inside her skull, adding to her growing queasiness. Bleaker's only full-time EMTs, Gary and Lew, showed up at her bedroom door and set up shop with their medical equipment at her feet. Instead of Chief Vance, Officer Danny Threen followed them.

"Ma'am, seems where you are today trouble goes." Gary teased her as he checked her pupils then listened to her heart. He moved on to check her throat and temple while Lew relayed the information to the doctor on duty at the hospital's emergency room.

"I'm fine," Lottie automatically protested while the two men examined her, and Keenan fussed behind them. She knew she was going to the hospital but hated to be such a nuisance. The town had enough to worry about.

"Mr. Waverly, what happened?" Threen pulled out a notebook and pen.

"Miss Ashley at the diner saw me and asked if I was headed in this direction. I told her I was so she asked if I'd bring this bag of food to Miss Lottie. I think she," Keenan nodded toward Lottie, "has an appointment to see someone and hadn't eaten. I didn't see anyone around when I got here so I rang the doorbell. When no one answered, I rang it again several times. I was about to leave, thinking I might have missed her when I heard a crash inside. Like glass breaking. I got worried. Thought maybe she fell. Could've been hurt, so I busted a window and came on in. Good thing, too. I called out and whoever had her must've heard me. Made a break for the back door apparently. That's the way she pointed." He led the officer down the hall to a door that was locked now. A corner of glass was broken though.

"The perp must have broken in, attacked Miss Amberville then ran out the same way." The officer squatted to get a better look at the glass. "The glass is broken inward." The deputy pointed out the shards lying along the hallway. "Bet there's glass leading away as well. That guy would have run back through it to get out." He unlocked the door then used the tip of his pen to pull it open wider and leaned forward. "Yeah, see in the cracks there on each side of those paving stones? I'll get my kit and dust for fingerprints and look for any tracks outside." When he turned, he exclaimed, "Miss Amberville! What are you doing out here? You belong in the ER."

Lottie stood not three feet away. She had heard the officer's comments and shivered, wondering if she'd ever be safe again. "I'm fine," she said weakly as the world faded from hazy gray to total black.

~ * ~

"You have no right to keep me here," Jud yelled as Vance walked away. His wrists ached from the short time his hands had been cuffed, a testament to how tightly the police chief had locked them.

"Sure I do." Vance stopped at the door and leaned against it, his attitude cocky, his voice low, sinister sounding. He rubbed the bridge of his nose and hooked a thumb in his belt. "I can hold you for seventy-two hours for suspicion." He didn't say anything else, but Jud could tell there was more to be said. Vance had that 'ask me' look on his face.

That gloating expression of confidence warned him that trouble stood not six feet away, but for the life of him, he couldn't put a finger on what Vance might think he had against him. So he had to give in to the man and ask. "Suspicion of what?"

"Well, actually I have more than suspicions. I have proof."

"Of what, damn it!" Jud grew tired of playing word games with this man.

"Murder."

The way he said that one word would have sent shivers down the spines of battle hardened soldiers. Jud was no different. "Who am I supposed to have murdered?" The faintest sheen of sweat dampened his upper lip; he could feel it. That itch in the middle of the back that meant danger to a soldier on active duty overseas started making itself noticed. Vance was gunning for him, but accusing him of murder was ludicrous.

"Mathew Jetter." Vance was enjoying this way too much.

Jud laughed aloud in relief. "Why would I murder him? He was my best friend."

"Yeah, right," Vance drawled. "You always threaten your best friend just before you get on a bus and ride away?" Once more he drew his finger down the length of his nose then hooked that finger over his pouched-out lips and cast his eyes up, as if thinking about what he just said. "Yep, you really know how to treat friends and family." In a complete change, he snorted and cast a glare at Jud. "Besides, I have evidence that says you did it."

A gasp escaped Jud. "Evidence!" He came to the bars and grabbed them in both hands, his anger rising, his frustration higher yet. "What kind of evidence do you think you have?"

"A handmade bone handled knife was sticking out of Mathew Jetter's back. The name J Longtree was carved into the handle."

Vance looked as smug as a lawyer who just found the smoking gun. He could see Jud in prison for the rest of his life for murder one.

"That knife? That was my dad's. He made it when he was a kid on the res. That J you think stands for my name is J for Jacob. Jacob Longtree. And I can tell you one thing, my dad did not rise from his grave to kill Mathew." At that point, getting a bit snotty with Vance wasn't going to make the man any madder.

Jud knew the knife the chief talked about, but it was in a display case at his mom's home. He hadn't seen it in twenty years. If Vance had that knife, then Mathew's death was no accident. Someone had murdered him and tried to blame it on Jud. And his mom was involved somehow. The acid in his stomach churned, the bile of fear now rising faster than his anger.

"Vance, I didn't kill Mathew, and I don't know who did. But someone might be after my mom. We need to protect her. Put a guard on her at the hospital." Jud rattled the bars enough to annoy the other man and bring him closer. "You may hate my guts, but Mom hasn't harmed anyone. Please, take care of her until I get out of here."

Obviously, Vance had missed the boat on that one; he must have forgotten Mary was hurt as well and might have information he needed. "Your mom's not going to cover for you, Longtree, but I'll put a man on her until she wakes up." Once more he moved to the door but stopped before walking out for real this time. "You killed Jetter. I have proof. You won't be getting out of here any time soon."

Not always in control of his emotions, this time Vance exercised supreme control; he slid the door shut so quietly that all Jud heard was the snick of the lock.

Helplessness crept into his soul. "Fathers of my people, I am Jud of the Cherokee. I ask no protection for myself but for Mary, your daughter. There is a mystery here. I must solve it and clear my name. I must do what Mathew Jetter told me to do before I left. Help us, Great Spirit."

~ * ~

Beep. Beep. Beep. *Did I leave something in the microwave?* Beep. Beep. Beep. *Is that the alarm on the oven? What was I baking?* Rustle. Beep. Rustle. Beep. Swish. Rustle. Beep. Swish.

Noises awoke Lottie. She squirmed, only to feel a sheet over her, a heavier blanket as well. Her eyes still closed, she took inventory of her situation. Sounds began to separate themselves into distinct patterns that she could identify.

Beep, beep, beep. *Is that a heart monitor?*

Rustle, rustle, rustle. The sound of the sheet as she restlessly moved her legs.

Swish, swish, swish. Air conditioning going on and off. Perhaps a fan in the room somewhere?

Her throat was so sore she could barely swallow. Lips parched, mouth cotton dry, she had no way to seek assistance here in the hospital. She had finally figured out where she was.

"Need something to drink?" A soft voice, a female voice, came from the bedside.

Lottie eased her eyes open to discover Ashley sitting beside her in a dimly lit room. And she held a cup with a straw. Oh, heavenly days, the idea of a drink sounded good! So she nodded; that's all she was capable of, and even that hurt.

Ashley held the cup close and set the straw in her mouth. One sip and Lottie knew that swallowing was not as easy as she hoped it would be. Her eyes slid shut, her energy as gone as that last sip.

"Hurts." She managed to get that one word out, though sandpaper coming up her throat wouldn't have hurt more.

"You have multiple bruises, but no broken bones. You're still alive, though I doubt you feel like it right now." Ashley whispered as if Lottie's ears were also injured.

Her ears were the only things that didn't hurt. And Ashley misunderstood. Lottie didn't want an inventory of her injuries; she just wanted to tell someone she didn't feel so great. She so seldom complained that this time no one recognized her word as a whine. Carefully she eased one arm up so she could press her fingers against her eyes. Doubt, like a wall of bricks falling on top of her, disabled her thinking, muddled her mind.

"Who?" Lottie wanted to know who tried to kill her. She rubbed her eyes and whispered around the palm of her hand. "Who?"

"Who tried to hurt you?" Ashley had spent so much time with the counselor-turned-friend-turned-mentor as they worked together on getting her equivalency diploma that she could practically read Lottie's mind. "Vance scoured your place for evidence but came up empty. Whoever did this came in through the back door. Must have thought to rob the place and didn't realize you were home. When you showed up, he attacked, then ran when Keenan showed up. But there was nothing left behind to show who did this." Ashley pushed the hair off Lottie's forehead and gave her hand a tender squeeze. "I have more than a few folks to call now that you're awake." Her sigh told Lottie there was someone she had to notify and did not relish the task. "I have to call Vance first though. He wants to interview you."

Vance. Vance. Vance. Like the beep of the monitor recording each heartbeat, Vance's name pattered through her mind in a mystical rhythm. There was something about him…

"Vance!" Lottie rose straight up in her bed like a specter from a grave, hollered his name then collapsed, clutching her throat, rolling, grimacing over the excruciating pain. She remembered what it was she wanted to tell the police chief. She didn't know who killed Mathew, but she knew who hadn't.

~ * ~

They never got around to questions about her attack, a robbery or motive.

"He's innocent." Lottie whispered, the only sound she could manage without tearing out her throat like she almost did earlier.

"And how do you know?" His hand wrapped around the bed rail so tightly that his knuckles blanched, Vance looked ready to explode.

"He was never out of my sight from six this morning until you saw him on the sidewalk, helping me break up that fight."

"And how the hell did you manage that? Did you two spend the night together?" His snide questions were insulting.

"Nothing so exciting, no." Lottie could see how tightly he clenched his jaw. The muscles at the side of his face fairly bulged with controlled fury. She took a sip from the large mug she held in order to give him time to calm down. "We just happened to be in the same place at the same time. I had a flat coming home from Spartanburg. Tire went out the other side of the cemetery. I live on this side, one block off Avenue A, so I decided to cut through the cemetery and go home. The flat could wait until daylight." Her throat protested such long speech, but she had to get Jud Longtree out of Vance's jail. "The last thing I noticed before turning off the engine and locking up was the time, five-fifty. It was plenty dark, but I'm not afraid, like some.

"I made my way through the woods and came out on the backside of Rest Haven. Fortunately, before Longtree saw me, I saw him. I could see his outline by the light of a small campfire he'd built next to a headstone." Her body protested lying flat so she powered the bed a little higher. Vance was less intimidating that way. "The guy sat cross-legged and talked, real low. But there was no one with him that I could see. Once in a while he'd sing, but I couldn't make out what." Lottie shrugged gingerly. "Well, occasionally I thought I heard snatches of the Beatles and Elvis, but there were plenty of songs I didn't recognize. I wasn't afraid so much as curious, so I watched."

How could she make a hard-ass like Vance understand how hypnotizing it was to watch a man while safely hidden in the night? "The sun rose, and I could see his profile. He'd turn occasionally, and I saw his face. I know who the man was now, no question about it. I was watching Jud Longtree. I couldn't see what headstone he sat by, but you can locate that campfire and find out. I bet it was his father's."

"So you just stayed and watched a stranger camped out, singing in a graveyard!" Vance's voice rose on a note of incredibility.

"Well, yeah. There wasn't any harm, and it was kind of interesting."

Vance opened and closed his mouth several times. Lottie marveled at how much he resembled the fish in the science aquarium at school but knew he wouldn't appreciate her comparison.

He took a belly-deep breath, let it out slowly then asked with a calm façade, "So what happened when he left?"

"I followed him. Wanted to see who he was. I walked on the other side of the street. He rounded the corner, but I was already at the far corner so I crossed the street behind him. When I saw the boys about to fight, I knew I was going to need his help. Those two are best friends, but that would have been a nasty fight. I've seen them wrestle, and I saw Peter Dansing box one time."

"And just where did you see him doing that, Missy?"

"That's beside the point, Chief Vance. Rumor has it that Mathew had been dead less than an hour when we found him. That true?"

She could tell he didn't want to confirm the rumor, but the truth would come out eventually, so he nodded.

"I was with Longtree for hours before that. He never left my sight. He's not your man. You have to let him go."

"The hell I do!"

"Find any blood on his clothes? Or his hands?" Her certainty of the man's innocence thrust deep into Vance's assumptions like that knife he found and twisted. "I'd guess not because he was nowhere near Mathew until we found him." Like the last drop of water in her mug drained away to empty, Lottie's energy faded before Vance's mounting rage. If unmitigated wrath were a smell, she knew her room would be swimming in aromatics right about then. He looked like he wanted to throw something. Or shoot someone. Any excuse might set him off, so she sank further into bed and closed her eyes. "Tell Longtree to stop by when he comes to see his mother."

Chapter Three

Trained by the best to endure in silence if necessary, Jud kept his mouth shut when Officer Threen escorted him out of the cell to the dressing room where he exchanged the orange jumpsuit for his camo uniform. At the processing desk, he signed papers and retrieved his belongings.

The most infuriating thing was that neither Vance nor Threen would tell him what happened. The only thing he had was a piece of paper. Room 113. That must be his mom's room.

Jud stepped on to the dark sidewalk and scanned Main Street. He checked the time. After nine. The earlier thunderstorm had washed away the mugginess and left spring freshness that cooled his face and helped flush resentment out of his system. A brisk wind carried the promise of a cool morning to come though.

Savoring a personal sense of freedom he'd never appreciated before, he donned his cap and set off for the hospital just down the block. The walk refreshed him after the tepid air conditioning in his jail cell.

He stopped at the nurse's station not far from room 113. "Excuse me? Where is the man that's supposed to be guarding my mom's door?" He could see the room, but no one was posted there. If Vance left his mom in danger, he'd have a few short and pointed words for the man.

"Curtis Warren is seated at her door, Sergeant." The nurse's assurance that someone was watching over Mary confused Jud.

40

"I don't understand. I was supposed to go to room 113. If that's not Mary Longtree's room, then whose is it?" His cap in one hand, with the other he waved the paper Threen gave him in front of Nurse Willows.

"Oh, that's Lottie Amberville's room." As if she had solved a great mystery, the nurse relaxed in her padded chair and beamed at him.

"What happened to her? She was fine last time I saw her this morning at the high school."

"You didn't hear?"

"No, I uh…" Jud set his face, let irritation simmer below the surface. "I was busy until a few minutes ago. So I don't even know how my mom's surgery went."

"Your mom is doing well. She's in a medical coma, but Doctor Latner will talk to you about that tomorrow morning." Willows turned sympathetic, willing to soothe a flustered family member.

Jud's relief wilted him for a moment; he leaned against the counter, eyes closed, one hand wiping the lines of worry from his face. Satisfied that his mom was in good hands, he thought of the woman he met that morning. "What happened to the counselor?"

"Miss Amberville came in after someone attacked her in her home. Could have been a burglar."

"Is she all right?" Jud tapped his fingers on the counter top, wondering why Vance directed him to Lottie first.

"She'll be fine. Bad bruises. Especially on her throat. Very sore. She'll probably go home Monday morning. The doctor wants to monitor her concussion for forty-eight hours." Willows shut the file she'd been writing in and put it on a pile at her elbow. "You're supposed to see her?"

Jud nodded once, then asked, "Is it too late to go in?"

"We usually discourage folks from visiting after nine, but I think it'll be okay this time. If she doesn't feel like having a visitor, she'll let you know." The woman stood and came around the end of the counter, then propped an arm on it. "My son is a sophomore and says the counselor is pretty outspoken. You never have to worry about where you stand with her." Her grin suggested that the young man might have had run-ins with his counselor so talked from experience.

"I'll just stick my head in and say hi then." Jud rapped his knuckles twice on the counter top and gave the nurse a farewell nod. "Thanks, ma'am."

"You're welcome. Oh, and your mother's room is down that hall," Willows said, pointing over her shoulder.

Jud eased the door open in case Lottie was asleep. Her eyes were closed so he started to leave, but she stopped him.

"What took you so long?"

He came into the small room and took up a position at the foot of her bed. "I came straight here from the police station."

"Took him long enough." Her fragile-sounding voice stirred him, and he was glad she still had her eyes closed. "I talked to him before five." Her sigh said she was sleepy.

"I'll just leave you now, miss. Can't imagine why Vance sent me over here." Jud turned to leave.

"Wait."

Her voice was so low he might have imagined her speaking.

"He didn't tell you, did he?"

He puckered his mouth and gazed back over her bed to the soft light on the wall. What was Vance up to now? How was this woman involved in his release? "He doesn't talk to me unless he has to."

"He might have this time." She rolled her shoulder and grimaced. Then opened her eyes.

Jud sucked in air through his nose and held it. For the first time, he got a good look at her. Too many things happening before prevented him from noticing the deep waves in her hair. The light seemed to weave in and out of it, bringing out highlights of what looked like deep red. Her dark brown eyes caught that same light and glowed, not supernaturally but with intelligence and charm, even though she lay banged and bruised. Skin the color of a milky latte sported purple spots, especially around her neck. Lost in the wonder of finally seeing her without interference, he temporarily forgot what she said. But when she cut her gaze up to his and frowned, he drew his mind away from her to what she'd said.

"Tell me what?"

"Why he couldn't charge you with murder." She wasn't being coy, he finally decided. She honestly thought the chief would inform him of something that important.

"Like I said, we don't talk. Why am I not in jail?"

"Because I told him you were in the cemetery when I saw you around six, and you never left my sight until we parted in the gym." She had the good grace to drop her gaze then. A blush warmed her cheeks as she folded the sheet over her stomach three times, unfolded it then repeated the folds again.

She saw him at his dad's grave? Watched him! Lord, the things she must have heard. He mentally went over what he'd said, while thinking himself alone in the night, safe from those who didn't want him. His practical nature told him the past was gone, and the present looked better than it had in hours. The future was still pretty murky though.

"Oh, I wasn't all that close. Couldn't really tell what you were saying or what you were doing. I just…watched." Lottie smoothed the sheet and stared at him. "I didn't have anywhere I needed to be, so just stayed. It was nice out there."

"Thanks for telling Vance. You could have kept quiet. You apparently don't think a lot of me. That's too bad. The public version of my life is not the same as the private one." He clasped his hands behind his back because he suddenly wanted very much to still her nervous hands.

"That's what Mathew told me once when I asked him about you."

"Listen, miss…"

"Listen, sergeant…"

They spoke at the same time and stopped just as suddenly, both overcome with embarrassment.

"Thanks for your help, Miss Amberville."

"Friends call me Lottie." She lowered her gaze again and twisted the top edge of the sheet. "Sergeant, I'm sorry I intruded on your privacy. But after what happened, I'm glad I did." The corner of her mouth lifted, and she let it flow into a full-blown smile. A yawn caught her by surprise. One hand quickly came up to cover her mouth. "Sorry, I'm a bit tired."

"I'll leave you then. Have to check on my mom." He moved to the door.

"Is she okay?"

"Still in a coma. I'll see the doctor tomorrow."

"Let me know what he says?" Another yawn stretched out her words.

Jud stopped halfway out the door. "Lottie, my friends call me Longtree—guys do anyway. You can call me Jud. I'll be back tomorrow."

"Promise?"

He wasn't promising her anything, so he quietly shut the door.

~ * ~

"Nothing happening here, Sergeant." Curtis Warren stood and shook Jud's hand when he approached. "Mrs. Longtree's been asleep since they brought her in. Doc's been by twice. Left instructions with me and the nurse to call if necessary. Otherwise he expects to see you here tomorrow at nine."

Jud slipped past the man into his mom's room. Perhaps it was small to begin with, but all the monitors crammed in there left little room for comfort. One chair stood squeezed tight against the rail. Jud pulled it out a bit by carefully moving a monitor or two, then sat.

He gave his mother as close a scrutiny as he did Lottie. "You're looking pale, Mom. Especially for a Cherokee." He took her hand and rubbed the tender skin across the back. "*U ni tsi*—mother—what happened? Did you see someone? Who killed Mathew?" His mother could hear him, he believed. If he asked now, she would be ready with an answer when she regained consciousness.

A fear welled up in him; what if his mother never woke up? Her face lay in slack repose, her hair tossed carelessly on the pillow, her arms tucked under the sheet, protection against the chill in the room. No pearl earrings, no big numbered watch—things he'd sent her along with pictures and stories. She refused to let him brood through the years. Mary knew how much he missed his dad. And Mathew Jetter. But did she know how much he'd miss her if she died?

Though she lay still as a stone, he knew she would admonish him for sitting here, hungry, worrying over her when he could do nothing. "Get a good night's sleep. Things will look better tomorrow," was one of her favorite sayings. Mary believed a night's peaceful sleep cured most ills.

He leaned forward, elbows on the bed, careful not to touch any wires or tubes. One long thick finger smoothed the finely chiseled skin on her cheek. "I think I'll head to the house. Need to check it out anyway. Vance said he has Dad's knife. Not sure what happened there, but I'll find out." Getting to his feet, he gave Mary a soft kiss then left, the long day and extraordinary circumstances finally catching up with him.

~ * ~

Jud approached his mother's home silently, though out in the open. Something odd was going on in Bleaker, and he wanted to know what it was, since people he loved were involved. Mathew was dead and his mother critically injured. At least Keenan was alive and well. That woman, Lottie, was safe though pretty beat up from what he could see. Thanks to his mom, he actually knew more about her than he let on. Mary felt it was her duty to keep him up on what was going on in town. Her letters included the latest news and local gossip—as if he cared.

Before entering the dark house, he circled the north corner, checking for bent branches on the ligustrum bushes—signs of a possible intruder. No windows were broken or opened until he got to the sheltered back porch. The light in a recessed corner was dark; the bulb lay on the deck. Rather than touch it and smudge any fingerprints, he left it lying. He leaned in closer to see a window screen was gone, and the top center windowpane busted in. The lock was undone, and the window was open.

Whoever took Jacob's knife had entered this way. The back door was still locked. Though the perpetrator was probably long gone, Jud took no chances. He unlocked the door and slipped in. Then he stood, listening. Croakers outside sang in mellow froggy voices. A few fireflies made their dot-dash way across the yard. All seemed normal.

On the balls of his feet, Jud made his way along the wall. Not one to assume the enemy was gone, he checked the house.

Finding no one, he returned to the kitchen and stood with hands on hips, one hand washing the weariness from his face. His stomach growled. "I need some light before someone calls the cops and tells them a burglar broke in." The first smile of the day eased across his face…just as someone hit him on the back of the head!

"Damn that hurt!" How long had he lain there? From his position on the floor, he opened his eyes and drew in a cringing breath. He just as quickly held that breath, afraid to suck in any more death-thick air. As fast as he could he stood, and in a jerky-sort of waltz made his way to the back door, opened it and left it that way. Holding the bump on the back of his head, he drew in a lungful of fresh air then made a mad dash back into the house. A prayer for his safety flitted through his mind as he turned off the four unlit pilot lights on his mom's old gas stove. The smell of gas almost made him gag, the fumes creeping through the shirt material he used to cover his mouth and nose.

By the time he returned to the far side of the yard, he could feel a headache tightening his nerves. Between the open door and broken window, enough air would circulate to disperse the fumes shortly. In the meantime, he had to let Vance know what happened.

He circled the house again and stood at the curb while pulling out his cell phone. "9-1-1, this is Jud Longtree. I am at 1620 Myers Street, my mom's home. Someone knocked me out and blew out the pilot lights on her gas stove. I was lucky to wake up with nothing more than a headache and the smell of gas in my nose. Could you send the fire department to check out the house? And send someone from the police department." If he was lucky, Vance would be home in bed and a different officer would take the report. He didn't get a chance to check on the glass case where his dad's knife had been on display for years. That was probably as shattered as the back window.

He no sooner got to the other side of the street than a fire engine and water truck turned the corner and pulled up next to the curb in front of the house. Firefighters tumbled out and began pulling on SCBA—

self-contained breathing apparatus—gear. They ignored him as they prepared to enter.

One man—the driver—approached Jud. "You Jud Longtree, the guy who called 9-1-1?"

"Yes, sir. Someone knocked me unconscious, but not for as long as they hoped, I think. I came to and smelled gas. My mom's stove is gas. All four burners were on, but the pilot lights were off. House reeks. The back door is open though, as well as a window next to it."

"We'll ventilate the house then check for damages. You should get to the hospital or call an ambulance."

Jud waved him off. "I'll live. Had worse. Besides, I see a police car coming. I'll have to give them my report."

The firefighter nodded then made his way back to his crew who were pulling huge fans from compartments along the engine's side.

The car pulled up next to him, and Jud groaned but not so much that Vance could tell. The chief got out of the car and surveyed the scene across the street. "What happened?" he yelled as he leaned against the car and watched the activity over the roof.

Jud approached but stopped shy of the car's front fender. He repeated his story about the house and someone knocking him unconscious. But for Vance, he added what he had discovered about the window and his suspicions that someone broke in specifically to steal the knife.

"So why did you get knocked out?" Vance's pen stopped in the middle of writing and shot Jud a nasty glare.

"No reason I can think of. Mom might be in danger, but I had nothing to do with murder." His head hurt now despite the fresh air. Made solving the mounting problems hard. "I'm no threat to anyone."

"Just my peace of mind and this community's," Vance muttered loud enough for Jud to hear. The police chief snapped his notepad shut, pocketed the pen and made his way to the trunk of the car. From there, he pulled out his crime scene bag. "Damn, I've used this more in one day than I ever have."

The same firefighter returned to Jud. He included Vance in his report. "House is clear, sir. The pilot lights were out like you indicated.

47

Back window's broken, but my guys didn't do it."

"It was broken before you got here. Guess who ever tried to gas me didn't realize some fresh air would come in through there. At least enough to save my life." Jud reached for the knot on the back of his head just as the fireman stepped up to him and put a hand out to stop him.

"I wouldn't do that if I were you. There's blood running down the side of your neck onto your camos. You really need to get to the hospital and have someone take a look at that."

"I'll go, but I have to get some clean clothes first." Jud avoided rubbing his head, but it wasn't easy. His headache had increased with Vance's questioning. He stopped the fireman though. "Can you do something about boarding up that broken window? I'd hate to leave and someone just walk in. My mom would kill me if I left the house open."

The fireman grinned and nodded as he ran a finger down the side of his face. "Yeah, know what you mean. My mom's like that, too. Sure, we can board it up. You have a key for the back door?"

"Yes, sir. What's your name?" Jud stuck out his hand, determined to do the right thing even if the people in the community wanted to think the worst of him.

"Frank Eddings." Frank shook Jud's hand, nodded to Vance and ran back to help his men load the fans.

Jud and the chief watched the engine pull out. "You have a car?" Vance wanted to know.

"Yes. I'm going to get a change of clothes and take them with me. I'll get someone to check out this wound then spend the night in Mom's room."

"Yeah, if they don't keep you in your own room," Vance clarified. "Go get your clothes. I'll drive you there. Don't want to go home then have to come back and work an accident when you and that woozy head wrap a car around a telephone pole."

Caught in a surreal moment, unable to believe Theo Vance of all people was actually being nice, Jud stood like a garden statue, his mouth hanging open. The odd thought hit him that maybe the lump on the back of his head had affected his hearing.

When he didn't move, Vance turned grumpy. "Go on, dang it. I don't have all night to cozy your ass. I'd like to get some sleep before something else happens and another citizen winds up in hospital."

Does he include me as one of those citizens, Jud wondered? But the energy-sucking Saturday had now turned into an exhausted early morning Sunday, and still he'd had no rest. Nor eaten. But his stomach was too tight to eat. So rest it would have to be. He'd missed meals before.

On legs that felt like pieces of thick wood, he made his way back into the house and retrieved slacks, shirt, underwear, socks and loafers from his room along with his shaving kit. He threw those, a clean towel and washrag into a duffle bag and locked up.

He returned to Vance's squad car where the chief held the back door open. "I'm not riding in front?"

"No one rides in front with a police officer. Even Walter rides in back the few times he rides with me in this car." By then, Vance had returned to his usual less-than-charming self and didn't look like he wanted to discuss the options. "Get in or walk. You're not driving in your condition." Vance stood sideways to Jud, his gaze on something in the distance. One hand held the door open, but he pushed it closed just a bit.

"I got the message. Thanks for the ride," and Jud slid into the back seat.

The four-block ride lasted about five minutes, seeing as Vance cruised slowly, checking out the storefronts. No one was out that late at night. The car stopped at the ER's double doors. A nurse stepped out. "You Jud Longtree?"

"Yes ma'am," Jud answered as he unfolded his tall frame from the back seat and hooked a hand through the duffle handle.

"Frank said you'd probably show up. Said he hoped so. That knot really bothered him since it was bleeding." She motioned with her head toward ER. "Get in, and let the doctor see you." She motioned him into a wheelchair waiting at her side.

"I don't really need that, ma'am."

"You want to get in these doors and get that headache taken care of tonight?" Her face went as stern as a drill instructor, leaving him no choice.

Jud tried to stare her down, but that didn't work. Besides his head did hurt. She could probably tell just by looking at him. Giving in to a superior rank in this case, he turned and gingerly lowered his body into the wheelchair, storing his bag on his lap, wrists crossed over each other on top. "See ya, Vance. Thanks." Glancing over his shoulder, he sighed, "Let's get this over with, Captain," he retorted, the nurse behind him chuckling as she pushed him inside.

~ * ~

"It's a slow night, Sergeant. Use the bathroom and clean up. I'd like to check you in for observation." Doctor Mackenzie held a prescription pad, writing out an order for pain pills. "You don't have a concussion, but I'm sure your head is pounding." He handed the paper over to Jud who stuffed it in his pocket.

"Thanks, Doc, but I don't do drugs. Of any kind. I'm not checking in either, but I'll be around." He gathered up his things, shook hands with the doctor and prepared to find a shower. "If you need me, I'll be in 105—my mom's room."

The shower refreshed him but made him sleepy by the time he got to Mary's room. Someone had squeezed a modified recliner in among the machines, and he gratefully sank into it for some rest. Which proved difficult as he unconsciously wanted to sleep on the side with the bandage. He used an extra pillow to wedge his head to the other side and eventually drifted off, the worries that plagued him no match for exhaustion.

~ * ~

Sunday morning began when two people showed up at the door to Mary's room. Chief Vance held the door open for Lottie. Jud checked the time: eight a.m. Seemed like he'd just gotten to sleep.

Because Lottie looked shaky, he evacuated the chair and practically pushed her in it. "Sit before you fall and tangle up Mom's wires," he joked sympathetically.

Though she rolled her eyes at his drollery, she sat without

resistance. "How's she doing?"

"Still unconscious. The doctor hasn't come by yet." He faced Vance and said in a mock conciliatory tone, "I'm not sure if this room will be big enough for all of us when he does." He made the pointed comment, hoping Vance would leave. The sight of a pretty woman early in the morning was enough to start the day right, but Vance's presence sucked the pleasure right out of Lottie being there.

"We'll worry about that when the man shows up," Vance said brusquely, as he moved further into the room, taking up personal space that made Jud want to shove him away. Since he wasn't one to back off from those trying to intimidate, he stood his ground until Lottie placed a hand on his arm and subtly pulled him back toward her chair.

"Mind if I wait with you for the doctor's visit?" She was entrenching her presence between the two men, and Jud recognized it though he didn't particularly appreciate the protection.

"Sure, no problem." He opened his palms outward, showing Vance he wasn't going to let the man get to him. If a hard glare could push the chief back then his should have, but Vance seemed impervious to subtleties.

The tension could have gotten worse, but the chief broke it by asking, "Why are the three of you in the hospital?" He waved away Lottie's outraged gasp. "What I mean is, in a matter of hours, Mary was hurt, Lottie, you were attacked, and so were you." He drew his back up straighter then leaned forward and pointed a pudgy finger at Jud. "This didn't happen until you came back to town," he accused and turned sideways as if Jud were an inferior person.

"Look, Vance..." Jud wanted to beat the shit out of the man for his insinuation, but the effort wasn't worth it. That feeling—being talked down to—that followed him everywhere in this town when he was young surged to the fore again. No sooner did he control his irrational emotions than he felt Lottie's hand again, this time her fingers twined in his.

"Chief Vance, the only thing Jud and I have in common is Mary. Other than that, there's nothing to make anyone think he caused Mathew's murder or my attack." As if Vance's words suddenly filtered through her bruised mind, she cut her glance up to Jud. "You were attacked?"

He could see the fear in her eyes as she also shot an anxious glance at Mary. God, he hated being the source of their injuries, but Vance might have a point. Was he the reason all this was happening?

"I went home last night after leaving here, and someone was waiting. Knocked me out and turned on Mom's gas stove. Minus the flames." He turned his head so she could see the bandage behind his left ear. "I'm fine now. Headache's almost gone. A cup of coffee'll fix that."

"If you two will focus back on the issue at hand here," Vance interrupted. "All three of you have something else in common. Mathew Jetter. But only one of you might have a score to settle." His hand cut the air between them but came up with his hand pointed at Jud. "You, Longtree." A dramatic silence fell that would have made the Immortal Bard proud.

While Shakespeare dealt with pompous kings, Jud only had to deal with one self-important police chief. "We've established that I didn't murder Mathew. Besides, that public display of hostility back on the day I boarded that bus was our way of getting me out of town before someone could shoot me. Mathew's idea."

Grasping the innuendo, Vance jumped on the idea of deception. "What the hell are you talking about?" His voice rose in loud demanding tones. Jud saw Lottie cringe at the noise in such a small room.

"Nothing that can be remedied years later. Someone had been taking pot shots at me. Mathew wanted me gone before they found the right range. So we staged the argument to make people think I wasn't coming back."

"You gotta be kidding!" Vance flung his arms wide, turned away from Jud and paced two steps to the door before he turned, his face scrunched up in thought. "That's the damnedest thing I ever heard. So you're saying you never had a reason to kill Mathew. You were friends?" By now, the man practically shouted.

Jud nodded once, unwilling to share with this arrogant man just how much of a father figure Mathew Jetter had become during the last few years he lived in Bleaker. That was personal. Vance didn't deserve 'personal' information. He glanced down to see that Lottie had, at some point, released her tight grip on his hand and now sat rubbing the fingers of one hand with the other. That and the slight narrowing of her eyes showed how nervous this confrontation made her.

Before Vance could whip up another accusation or Lottie rub the skin off her hand, a doctor stepped through the doorway. He must have sensed the tension immediately as well as recognized Vance's bulldog-like expression. One of the disadvantages of living in a town with such a small population is that everyone knew everyone else and knew when to back off or put themselves forward as a buffer.

This man threw himself into the fray with a calm 'good morning' to Vance, a smile for Lottie and a handshake for Jud. "I'm Doctor Latner. I did Mrs. Longtree's surgery. I'd like to go over her prognosis with you." As smoothly as glass, Latner turned back to Vance and added, "If you'll wait outside, Chief."

Knowing he was dismissed, but Lottie Amberville was allowed to stay, Vance pinched his lips together so hard they went white. His tanned face flushed a dull red, but he refrained from saying anything...with obvious effort, as far as Jud could tell.

He worked to keep the stoic expression on his face, afraid that if he smiled, Vance would go ballistic on them in the tiny room. But seeing the man put in his place—even if only temporarily—satisfied his need for justice.

"I'll check back with you two later. I've got work to do." Vance couldn't slam the door. That would be unprofessional. Besides the door glided closed on pneumatic pressure. He settled for slapping on a poker face, balling his hands into tight fists and giving them an authoritative 'humph' before leaving.

Once the door closed though, Jud released the smile he'd been hiding. However, Lottie called him to task for it. Seemed she could practically read his mind. "That's not going to help...you laughing at him."

"But you have to give me credit. I did wait until he left." Jud stuck both hands in his pants pockets and rocked back on his heels. Confidence filled him and apparently oozed out of him because Lottie snorted.

"You're so bad. Vance's going to get you some day for something trivial, and he's not going to be nice about it. Probably something like jay-walking."

Doctor Latner was the one who humphed this time in suppressed laughter. "While we might enjoy the man's choler, we should get on to Mrs. Longtree's condition. I have other patients to see."

Lottie pushed her way out of the deep chair and stood. "I need to get to my own room. If doctors are making rounds, then my own should be by soon."

"You can stay, Lottie." Jud stepped forward with a hand out, about to stop her, but she raised a hand and waved goodbye.

"You can come by and tell me what he said later. And bring some coffee, would you? Real coffee. The stuff they have here is awful."

~ * ~

Sunday mid-morning and Jud hoped few would be in the diner so early. The visit with the doctor had gone well. He and Latner came up with a scheme to keep his mother safe for as long as possible. Between their plan and Curtis sitting outside her door, he hoped she'd be all right. However, the doctor had cautioned that she could wake at any time, and she might or might not remember anything about the accident.

Jud could only hope her fall was accidental, and no one was hoping she either died or was left alone long enough to murder. He settled on a stool in the quiet diner, his mind still going over what the doctor had shared.

"Good morning."

The voice came from somewhere to his left. Jud turned to see the blonde from yesterday standing near him, a little boy holding her hand, his neck craned back, looking up at him, the tiny glasses wrapped around his ears in danger of falling off.

"Good morning. Ashley, isn't it?"

Her smile lit up the area where they stood. Seldom had he seen such a dazzling display. One-hundred watts of pure joy, if he could compare such.

"Ashley Johnson." They shook hands, and she took the stool next to him at the diner's counter. The little boy sat on her lap, his elbows on the slick surface, his hands supporting his head and turned at such an angle that his neck had to hurt. Big blue eyes solemnly watched Jud. Unlike his mother, the boy never cracked a grin. "This is Cooper." She patted the boy on the hip and whispered, "Say hi to Mr. Longtree."

Cooper showed evidence of having Down Syndrome, slanting eyes, short broad hands, a flat nose bridge and a slightly smaller than expected head. His tongue stuck out ever so slightly. Whatever his condition, Ashley loved him. That was plain to see in the adoration of her gaze.

"How come your skin is red?" Trust a child to ask what's on his mind, no matter the consequences. Cooper blinked and peered through his thick glasses and a strand of blond hair hanging across his eyes.

"Cooper Johnson! What kind of question is that?" Ashley sounded mortified, her eyes wide, pleading for Jud to understand. Her son's question embarrassed her.

Honesty was the only way to handle the child, especially one who probably suffered from a mental disability. "I'm a Native American." He knew the label might mean nothing, but he wanted to see how the boy reacted.

"Naf Marcan?" The kid wrinkled his nose and blinked again. "What's that mean?" He scooted as close as he could, considering he sat on his mother's lap. Ashley obligingly turned the tall stool so the two were face-to-face.

Jud repeated what he said then added, "I'm an Indian."

Now he could see that Ashley's joy of life dwelled in her son as well. He evidently knew what an Indian was. The little boy's face lit up, and his smile was as charming as his mother's. "Wow, that's cool." He beamed at Jud then leaned forward as if to share a secret. "I know an Indian."

"You do?" Jud played along, knowing whom he would name.

"Miss Mary. She comes to our school sometimes and talks with Mr. Waverly. They make funny eyes at each other, too." He leaned back and rested against Ashley's chest. "I like Miss Mary."

"Can you like me, too? I'm Miss Mary's son. Just like you are your mama's son."

Cooper considered that for a few seconds before nodding. "Us sons gotta stick together," he stated solemnly. A frown set in across his small brow. "Can I be an Indian, too, so we can be alike?"

"Sorry, little man. I'll be the Indian, and you can be my friend. Okay?"

"Sure thing!" Satisfied that all was well in his world, Cooper turned his attention to the glass of milk the waitress put in front of him.

While the boy sipped his drink, Jud turned his attention to Ashley. "You're Lottie's friend. Have you seen her yet? She never said when she could go home." The waitress interrupted to ask him what he'd like. He gave her a to-go order for a large breakfast with two large coffees.

"One of those for Lottie?" Ashley acknowledged her fellow waitress who set a large and small plate in front of them.

"She asked if I'd bring one. Said the hospital coffee was terrible." He didn't blush but felt like he might.

"She loves coffee. Must come from her background. I swear the woman has coffee running through her veins."

"Really." The comment piqued his curiosity, but he wasn't about to ask for details.

"Yeah, you should get her to tell you about her relatives sometime. Though she doesn't usually go into that sort of stuff with strangers." Ashley talked as she cut up pancakes on Cooper's plate. "But then she rarely takes to strangers so fast that she lets them call her by her first name." She fluffed the little boy's hair tenderly. "There you go, baby. Chew each bite before swallowing."

"Where's Mr. Johnson this morning?" Jud pulled out his wallet and handed some bills to the waitress. He immediately noticed the quiet next to him.

"There's no mister in our family. Just me and Cooper. He left after

Cooper was born. Said he wasn't sticking around to help." Ashley spoke in a matter-of-fact voice as if having no husband was not a big deal. But the pain in her large eyes belied that. Raising a son might give her joy, but raising a child with disabilities was a challenge for a single mother. And to be single because a man deserted his family was worse.

Jud wanted to kick himself for bringing up bad memories. "I didn't mean to remind you of something painful."

The model-beautiful woman appeared fragile for a second before collecting her dignity. "I've put it behind me. Happened a long time ago, and I got the best of the deal." She kissed Cooper on the ear, and he let out an 'ooh, Mom' before trying to wipe the kiss away. Jud could have told him that once a mother bestowed a kiss on her child, there was no wiping it away.

Fortunately for the awkward situation Jud found himself in, his order arrived just as the Johnsons finished their breakfast.

"Are you on your way to the hospital?" Ashley paid her bill and used the sweat off her water glass to dampen a napkin and clean Cooper's mouth and hands.

"Thought I would before the coffee and my breakfast get cold." He folded over the top of the sack that held the coffees and food.

"We'll walk with you. I'm on my way there now."

"Are we going to see Miss Lottie now?" Cooper bounced on the balls of his feet between his mom and Jud.

"Sure are. We're going to walk there with Mr. Longtree." Ashley took his hand and led the way out the door to the sidewalk.

"Are you a long tree?" Cooper once more asked in childish wonder.

Ashley had the grace not to laugh at her son or scold him. "That boy can embarrass me to no end sometimes. The things he comes up with."

"No, that's my name." Though Jud smiled, he stopped to think about how the boy perceived the name. Because Cooper was so short, he stood with his head far back so Jud went down on one knee next to the boy. "Well, I guess someone thought I was as tall as a tree. But you can call me Jud. Your mother, too. How's that?"

"Sure thing, Jud." Cooper took one of Jud's hands when he stood then grasped one of his mother's. "Can we go see Miss Lottie now?"

"Sure thing," Ashley and Jud said at the same time, the unison affirmation making them smile in friendship.

The sun wasn't summer time warm yet, but they walked at the little one's speed despite the coffee and food Jud carried that was probably getting cold. While Cooper did a bit of window-shopping, Ashley and Jud visited. "Lottie is my teacher. I never finished high school. My dad died, and I went to work to pay bills. Old story— happens all the time to lots of people. But I did regret not getting that diploma. Once Cooper and I shook loose of Mr. Johnson and settled here, Lottie volunteered to help me. I got my diploma last year. Now she helps me with online college classes. There's just about nothing I wouldn't do for that woman."

"I'm impressed."

"Yeah, she's something else, isn't she?" Ashley accepted Jud's praise on her friend's behalf.

"I'm sure Lottie is a fine person, but I meant you. I'm impressed with your efforts to make a better life for yourself and your little boy." He shifted the food bag to his other hand, while his eyes signaled her. To the little boy's delight, they held Cooper's hands and swung him up between them. His squeal of delight set them to laughing.

"Thanks for the compliment, Jud. I guess I'm like all mamas. I want my baby to have better than me. And Lottie Amberville's the person who's helped me do that."

They entered the shady hospital foyer and turned toward room 113.

"I want to get this coffee to Lottie before it gets cold," Jud explained above Cooper yelling to a nurse he knew.

Ashley hushed the boy. "Quiet, Coop, or they'll throw us out, and we won't get to see Lottie." She pushed the door open a little and stuck her head in. "Ready for company?"

Whatever the answer, she pushed on through, Jud following in her wake. Cooper busted in shouting, "Miss Lottie, guess what?"

"What?" Lottie sat up in bed as they entered and went along with the little boy's guessing game.

"Jud's an Indian! He said we're sons. Ain't that neat!" Cooper tried to climb on the bed with Lottie, but Ashley pulled him off. "Don't, Cooper, and don't yell. Remember what I said."

"Oh yeah, but ain't that something, Miss Lottie. A real Indian."

While Lottie hugged Ashley and smiled at Jud, she reminded Cooper of something he forgot. "But, Coop, you've seen Indians before. Remember when we went to the Indian Reservation with Miss Mary and saw the dances?"

Hum, interesting! Lottie's been to the res with his mom. Jud wanted to know more about that trip, but Cooper was doing the talking.

"I 'member. But they were dressed up in feathers. That ain't real Indians!" he proclaimed. "Jud is a real one. He's my Indian." Like the innocent that he was, he turned to his mother and implored, "Can I keep him?"

Ashley sputtered and held back most of an appalled groan. "Cooper Johnson, Jud is not a puppy! We can't keep him! Now you sit in that chair and stay quiet." When he started to say something else, she held a finger up to him and sternly pointed to the chair. Giving in to temporary defeat, Cooper clambered into the chair and sat, his thick lips open, his glasses sliding down the bridge of his nose.

"Oh, heavens, Jud. I am so sorry. I don't know what goes through his mind some times."

Before Ashley broke down and cried—tears welled in her eyes, and Jud knew she'd bawl any minute—Lottie broke the silence with "Coffee!"

In a quick diversion that he welcomed, she practically pounced on the large cup he handed to her. One sip and he forgot about Ashley's concern. Only a major sexual experience could make a woman look as satisfied as Lottie did. Her eyes rolled back then closed. She sank in the sheets and savored the brew to the exclusion of the three. "Heavens above but that's good!" As if she suddenly remembered that she wasn't alone, she eased her eyes opened and gave Jud a grin so filled with covert meaning that he almost became lightheaded. "You didn't happen to sneak in any extra food, did you?"

"I got a large order. I'll share. I think there's a knife in here. I can leave part of it for you." Jud raffled through the bag, bemused by the way she so easily captured half his breakfast.

"You aren't going to stay and eat with me?" Lottie's hand went to her throat, perhaps the coffee burned as she swallowed, but Jud could almost swear that she wanted him to stay and worried that he might leave.

A heartbeat passed between them before Jud gave her a gentle smile. "Sure, if it won't be a bother."

"No bother. You don't want to eat alone, do you?" Lottie perked up as soon as he gave in.

"Not particularly. Let me go check on Mom first though. You can divide the food. I'll be right back."

As the door closed at his shoulder, he heard one of the women say, "Damn, that's one hot Indian!" He couldn't tell which woman spoke. He supposed it was Ashley, but hoped it might have been Lottie.

Chapter Four

When Jud returned to Lottie's room, Ashley and Cooper were gone.

"They went to church. Ash said she's come by later and see your mom when Cooper is taking his nap at Sally's house. Say, that coffee hit the spot, Jud. I could use another, but I'm not asking you to go back to the diner." She caught his glance and fluttered her eyelashes. "But I won't stop you if you wanted to go."

While he eased into the chair by her bed, he cocked a small smile and muttered, "Maybe later."

She could tell he was uncomfortable by the way he shifted on the hard padded surface and would no longer look her in the eye. Just to push his button a bit, she leaned over and patted his hand. He didn't jerk away, but that's only because he caught himself in time. He did give her a quick glare that she chose to ignore. Mary told her once that Jud didn't make friends easily. Appeared that Mama knew best.

"I saved your breakfast, but it wasn't easy. Cooper wanted to eat it. The boy is a bottomless pit." She pushed the bedside table over to him: his breakfast sandwich and hash browns were still wrapped. Steam wove its way out of the coffee cup. "Eat up."

While he took a long drink of coffee and opened the sandwich, she sat up straighter, her interest in him stronger now than ever before. Curiosity ate at her, but warred with a tingly sensation at just watching the man eat. Lord, she wanted a relationship, but not with just anyone. Lottie tamped down her primitive urges and gave into the curiosity.

61

"You've been gone for years. Why'd you come back now?" Her body relaxed, she sat at eye level with him. No need to push for an answer. If she appeared too interested, he might shy away.

Several moments passed while he ate without answering. She kept her composure, certain that he would. As a counselor, she read body language well, enough to discern what kind of person someone was in that first meeting. Jud was one of those quiet guys. He focused on one thing at a time, if he had the opportunity. Right now, his breakfast was the object of his attention; maybe he was wondering what to tell her.

Lottie struggled with her natural tendencies to talk and fidget. Her sore muscles still protested fast movement, and the stillness of the room drove her nuts. She could understand his distress over his mother's condition, but she really wanted that intense focus on her. If only for a little while. Just as she made up her mind that he was never going to share why he returned, he crumpled the paper, took the last sip and ditched all the trash in the can by her bed. Finally, he sat back in the chair and crossed his arms over his stomach, one ankle over a knee.

Ah, his attention had now shifted from a full belly to some other topic. She hoped she was that topic.

"Who killed Mathew Jetter?"

That certainly was a new topic, but not one Lottie expected. She gave in graciously, ready to brainstorm about the death—murder—of a friend and colleague. "I don't know." Her hope was that Vance, as aggravating as he was, might come up with clues as to who killed the principal. "Does Vance have any leads?"

"If he does, he's not sharing 'em with me. He really wanted to pin that on me, but then you came along. Now he's got to do the job this town pays him for." Jud spoke as nonchalantly as if they were discussing flowers.

"The question is, who benefits, as they say, from Mathew's death?" Lottie hitched higher until she sat with one leg bent beneath the sheet and the other hanging off the bed. As she thought, one foot swung back and forth, barely missing Jud's leg.

"He has no family. Nor a paycheck that would make anyone greedy. Or a position that anyone in their right mind would want."

Lottie ticked off her ideas on one hand. "Besides, everyone liked him."

When Jud's eyebrow lifted a fraction, she rolled her eyes up in disgust. Her assumption was wrong. "Okay, so someone didn't like him."

"Do you know of anyone with a grudge against him?

"Mathew was a private man. You probably remember that. He rarely said anything derogatory about anyone." She flopped back on her pillow and squeaked when her abused body protested. "Ouch!" Discouraged, she stared at the ceiling, for once forgetting Jud Longtree. "Maybe he did something to one of the kids, and he—or she—wanted revenge. Nothing pisses off a high school kid like being embarrassed."

Jud pulled his body straight and leaned forward, hands clasped between his knees. "Let's deal with that for a minute. Vance will be looking for the same thing we are, someone with a motive who had an opportunity to kill Mathew when no one was around." He quirked his eyebrows up then down. "Mom was there, but what she saw or not, no one knows. Perhaps the murderer doesn't know she was around."

He really believes that. I hope he's right. Otherwise, Mary is in trouble, Lottie realized. "Someone guarding her…just in case she was seen?"

He nodded, but frustration washed his face in worry. "She's as safe as we can make her. Right now though, we have to find out who the murderer is before that person strikes again."

"Right." She smacked a fist on the sheet hard enough to make it fluff.

"So let's go over who Mathew has dealt with recently as far as discipline goes." Jud's gaze scanned the room.

Lottie followed where he looked but couldn't tell what he wanted. "What are you looking for?"

"I need to make some notes. Got any paper?"

"None here, but I bet the nurse will loan you a pen and some paper." Lottie sent him off to gather what he needed that would help him see the big picture.

He entered the room, clicking the pen in agitation. "Let's get some names here." He drew a line down the center of the page. "We'll call this column 'Revenge'. Who has Mathew had run-ins with at school?" His hand poised, his gaze held hers steady, his assumption that she had answers to his questions.

"Hey, wait a minute. I can't tell you kids' names!" She held up a hand to ward him off. Her stomach went tight as if her credibility were in question.

"Look, Lottie. Kids talk. At least they did when I went to school. Who came into his office and what punishment they received is a matter of record. Who came and went in your office is too but not what you guys talked about." He let that acknowledgment soak in for a second then continued. "So did someone get back at him for that penalty?"

"When you say it like that, I suppose it's all right to tell you who he's had trouble with lately." She crossed an arm over her stomach and curled her fingers around her chin. "Umm, Sharon Eddings skipped school so many times that Mathew sent her before the juvenile judge. Sharon has to do a hundred hours of community service."

Jud whistled low and soft. "Man, that's a lot of missed free time. She had to be pissed over that." He made a note beside her name on his list. "Anyone else?"

"Let's see, Russell Cromwell was sent to in-school suspension for the rest of the year for bringing a hunting knife on the bus and into the school. He's a good kid, and I know he just forgot to take it out after camping. But hey," she shrugged and held her hands out, palms up, "I don't make the laws. I just try to help the kids cope with them."

"So Russell has lost his free time as well. No socializing *during* school time for him."

"That's right, and he has a girlfriend too. They walk to class all the time."

"Not any more they don't." Jud scribbled more notes then shot her a look demanding more names. "Who else?"

"The only other one I can think of is Peter Dansing." She was so busy concentrating on the kids and their disruptions that she almost missed Jud's contemptuous grin. "What?"

"Peter, the mayor's son? The one in the fight yesterday? What happened to him?" This time Jud acted like a vampire who just spotted a maiden with an available neck, standing alone, holding a sign saying 'free lunch'.

"I don't know what you and the mayor had going on in the old days, but he's an all right guy. His son stays out of trouble for the most part, but he slugged John Chambers last week and wouldn't say why. Mathew had no recourse but to suspend him for a week. He missed baseball practice and a game. He really was steamed over that."

"Anyone else?" He read over his notes while she thought.

Lottie loathed the idea that one of the kids might have killed Mathew. She hoped they all had good alibis. She caught movement out of the corner of her eye and saw Jud watching her expectantly. The sigh that escaped her was one of finality tinged by a touch of longing. He really was a handsome guy.

"No, that's it. The kids are pretty good here. Other than…" She stopped and pursed her lips. Would she be breaking confidentiality with her boss if she repeated a concern of his? No, she concluded. Mathew was dead, and anything that helped catch his killer was fair game.

Jud sat silent for a few seconds then cocked his head and asked, "When we broke up that fight, you mentioned the town had enough problems without the boys fighting. What'd you mean?" He was fast to realize her words had a deeper meaning. His face reflected an eagerness she didn't share. And spooked her a bit when he practically read her mind.

"Mathew called me in a week ago and asked me to watch the students. A few had been acting unusual. Had all year. But whenever any of us talked with them, they seemed all right. It was like trying to track down a wind about to turn into a tornado. Something's wrong, but you can't figure out what. Trouble but no way to figure out what kind. He wanted me to keep an eye open for possible drug use. He specifically mentioned drugs, and he'd never done that before though the word 'steroid' did pop up once. During the week, I'd go to his office to discuss something, and he'd be gone, walking around campus. He often walked the halls. The kids were used to seeing him. But now it seemed like he was looking for something, searching almost."

"Do you think somebody was doing drugs on campus?" Jud left the chair and wandered to the window.

Sunlight spilled through the blinds, and Lottie wondered how death could overshadow the brightness pouring through. The day was not beautiful no matter how sunny it was, however. "I have no proof or even suspicion. Mathew never told me anything."

"Did you notice any students acting out of the ordinary?" He talked to her over his shoulder, not bothering to turn.

"Yes. I turned their names over to Mathew and left. I was to speak at a counselors' conference Thursday and Friday. Naturally, my workshop was the last one Friday so I caught a couple of hours sleep and drove home early. I wanted to meet with Mathew Saturday morning and see what he had come up with. My car had a flat, and I walked home, only to find you in the cemetery." Lottie let her words ease off, afraid that Jud would make something of her spying on him.

He turned back to gaze out the window, his hands deep in his pockets. A frown marred his forehead. The tightness around his lips almost distorted their appeal. "Vance can come up with a perfect suspect, you know." He spoke so calmly that she couldn't imagine to whom he referred.

"Who?"

"My mom."

"No way! I know Mary Longtree wouldn't kill Mathew!" Incensed, Lottie swung her feet over the side and stood though she kept a hand on the mattress.

Jud grinned at how fiercely she protested his comment. Not for a moment did he think his mom killed Mathew, but he wanted to see what this woman thought. In an unguarded reaction, he knew. But now he had to placate her anger.

Holding both hands in front of him as a peace offering, he closed the gap between them and gently grasped her shoulders. Beneath his palms, she shivered, not from cold, but from indignation. He could tell. "Lottie, I was just saying what Vance has to be thinking. Though how she could harm Mathew then end up injured like that is anyone's guess." He slowly pushed her down until she sat fully on the mattress.

Watching her eyes in case she objected, he eased down, picked up her legs and swung them back into bed. Rather than flip the sheet over her, he pulled it up and smoothed it at the sides. No way was he touching her any more than he had to! That was just too much temptation.

As he leaned over her, the door behind him opened, and a deep voice said, "Well!" with as much subtlety as a ton of falling bricks. Jud shut his eyes for a second, shook his head and wished Vance to some deserted island. He could only assume that Lottie could read his thoughts or his expression because she grinned but quickly covered her mouth to avoid giving her merriment away. Vance would surely think she was laughing at him. As he straightened, Jud winked at Lottie. *Partners in conspiracy.*

"Morning, Vance. What do you want?" Jud wasn't going to play games with the man so got right to the point.

"I'm not here to see you, Longtree. I want to interview Miss Amberville. You can leave." *Nothing delicate about him.*

Lottie opened her mouth to protest, but Jud cut her short. "I'll go check on Mom. See you later." He let his fingers trail down the sheet as he walked past Vance. He could have warned the officer to go easy on her, but Lottie wasn't as weak as she appeared.

He left to the sounds of Vance asking almost the same question he had: who killed Mathew. Despite their headwork, he knew Lottie would be obligated to tell the police chief exactly what they had come up with, though he hoped she didn't mention his name, just acted as if it were all her idea. To his surprise, when he pushed open the door to his mother's room, someone was already there. For some reason, he thought no visitors would be allowed. The woman looked familiar, but he couldn't place her. She stood by the bedside, near the IV stand, a paisley shawl over one arm, her purse over the other. From the way she was dressed, he'd guess she had just come from church.

"May I help you?" He stepped to the end of the bed.

She had seen him come in, shifted her shawl to her left arm over her purse and held out her hand. "I'm Julie Dansing. Mayor Dansing is my husband." They shook, and Jud liked her firm handshake.

"Don't I know you?"

"We were in school together. I dated Jack in my junior and senior years. We were always together. I think you were a freshman when we were juniors." A smile settled on her face as if she were welcoming a new business for the Chamber of Commerce. "Jack had a meeting this afternoon and asked me to stop by and check on Mrs. Longtree and Miss Amberville." She came around the bed and stood next to Jud.

The men in his squad would have described Julie Dansing as tall, tanned and toned. Her sleek muscled arms were a becoming shade, and she was taller than Lottie by several inches. Her dark hair hung in soft waves to her shoulders. Her face could have been an ad for the All-American Girl.

"Pleased to meet you." A tingle of excitement went through Jud, but not the same as with Lottie. This woman didn't set off sparks of lust; she simply exuded a breath of fresh air attitude.

"With the principal dead and the counselor injured in the hospital, I'm sure the school will be unsettled tomorrow. I wanted to extend my sympathies but let my son know how the ladies were doing so he can help calm the others." She paused with one hand on the door and gave him a sad smile. "All of this..." she daintily stretched out her hand toward his mother, "leaves me nonplussed." Her face bore the strain of tragedy. "My husband and Mathew were close. Jack is taking this poorly."

Her words hit Jud hard. No one had yet asked him how *he* was coping with Mathew's death. The two men had shared letters and phone conversations, advice, emails and laughter for years. If anyone could have stepped in and taken his father's place, it would have been Mathew Jetter. Jud missed him with an aching heart and fierce determination to avenge his death.

"I understand his feelings, Mrs. Dansing. Thank you for coming by." He held up one hand in an informal salute as she slipped quietly out of the room.

He leaned over his mother and kissed her forehead just below the bandage that swathed her head. "Hi, Mom. You had a guest. Too bad you slept right through her visit. Nice lady." Despite his upsetting return to town, he acknowledged that a few nice people lived in

Bleaker.

~ * ~

"This the fire Lottie told me about?" Vance had his notebook out again and held a camera.

"Yes." Hands in his pockets, feet crossed at the ankles, Jud leaned against an oak tree not far from his father's gravestone. He was only answering whatever Vance asked; volunteering information wasn't in his plans.

"When did you get here?" Vance moved to one side, stooped over and snapped a few shots showing the campfire in relation to the headstone.

"I came early Saturday morning. I didn't check the time, though Lottie did."

"Why did you come?"

"Wanted to talk to my dad." Jud suspected Vance would want to make something of that, but to his surprise, the chief asked nothing else.

"I'm going to walk on through the woods to the road and take a few pictures of Lottie's car."

"I'll wait here." Jud straightened and moved closer to the grave.

Vance had parked his squad car nearby. He'd have to come back this way to get it. "Suit yourself," he said as he took off into the taller grass at the edge of the cemetery.

When Jud could no longer hear him lumbering through the underbrush, he let his shoulders relax. A bee buzzed past his ear, and he swatted at the noise before bending to pluck several weeds from the grave. Another buzz flashed by his head, this time whistling, an odd clucking sound behind him. His battle sense suddenly kicked in. He made a dive for the back of the tall headstone. One last buzz—a bullet—ricocheted off the stone not two inches from his head, the bullet lodging in a charred piece of wood in the fire pit.

Trained to seek out snipers, Jud scanned the cemetery and surrounding woods. Judging the angle from the tree where the first bullet miraculously missed him as well as the angle when he bent and this last one, the shooter had to be to the northeast, secure in a dense stand of underbrush so thick that even deer couldn't pass.

He needed to move rather than stay pinned down, had to find that shooter. As he squat-ran to the nearest tall headstone, memories from years ago flashed by, scenarios similar to this one. Shots, but no evidence. This time he could prove someone tried to kill him. Vance had pictures of that pile of burned wood; none of them showed a bullet hole. Forensics could possibly match that fragment to a gun.

When no further shots came, he ran bent over, quickly moving through the cemetery to the woods—a long twenty yards. From tree to tree, he maneuvered until he got to the area where he estimated the sniper had hidden. He took greater care now, not willing to wipe out a print or destroy evidence.

His concentration on the ground and brush was so great that at first, he didn't register the crashing sounds coming up behind him. When he realized what they were, he called out so Vance wouldn't shoot him by mistake. "Over here! Someone took some pot shots at me from this area. I'm looking for casings or material. Anything that might give me some idea who it was."

Vance pulled up beside him, puffing from his run. "I heard shots. You okay?"

"Yeah, just pissed." Jud pulled back a branch with exquisite care and leaned down to investigate the ground. "Lucky, too. All three bullets missed. There's a fragment in one of the logs at the campfire." He jerked a finger over his shoulder. Frustrated, he squatted with both arms resting on his knees. "No tracks. Too many leaves and needles covering the ground." He started to get up then paused. "Wait a minute…" He bent almost over on his head, peering under a thick bush. "Got a pencil or pen?" One long arm came back, hand out.

No telling what Vance was thinking, but he put his ballpoint pen in Jud's hand. Jud could almost feel the man breathing down his neck.

"Here." He passed the pen back to Vance. A bullet's copper jacket rattled on top of the pen. "Three shots. He must have found the other two casings easily enough but didn't have time to search for this one."

Vance pulled a small plastic bag from his pants pocket and slipped the casing in. He scribbled information on the outside and put it in his shirt pocket. "Now why the hell would anyone want to kill you?" He led the way out of the heavy brush and stopped. "You just got into town, and all hell has broken loose," he growled. "Why didn't you stay gone?" He made a beeline for his car. "I'll see if I can get any info on this. Ernest can take it to Spartanburg." He still muttered as he rounded the fender and opened the door. "You better get out of these woods." Vance never offered Jud a ride home. His tires threw gravel as the car spun away.

Another car coming in passed the black and white going out. The driver must have seen Jud and veered to a stop in the spot Vance had vacated. A tall man got out, a business type, with stylishly cut graying hair, white long sleeve shirt with cuff links and politically correct blue tie. The only thing missing was the suit coat which Jud could see folded over the passenger headrest.

His heart just now slowing after the shooting incident, Jud wondered if his day was getting better or worse. The man coming toward him was none other than the mayor of Bleaker, Jack Dansing. High school asshole.

Where Julie Dansing shook hands with him, Dansing approached Jud without offering his hand. "Longtree, long time no see."

Both men stared at each other. Dansing didn't look bored; he looked relaxed, open and amenable to business, except for the lack of that handshake. He stood firm, his gaze direct, his face devoid of emotion. In fact, Jud thought he looked just a little too relaxed, his pose practiced, too calm. Dansing wore the air of a confident man. But was he as self-assured as he appeared?

"Dansing." Jud nodded once. Like Vance, he wasn't making himself a target for someone's cheap shots. Verbally or otherwise. Someone had already tried that today. He counted himself lucky to be alive; the shooter hadn't found his range. While he waited for Dansing to do something, he brushed dirt off his shirt and slacks and ran his hands through his hair. Short as it was, he still managed to gather a few thin twigs.

"Running through the woods again?" Words with double

meanings, old taunts.

"I'm a big boy now. All grown up. I don't run anymore. I seek."

"Find what you were looking for?" Dansing stuck his hands in pockets and rocked back ever so slightly.

"Not yet." Jud wasn't about to leave and put his back to this man. "But I will." Memories of jeers and being the butt of jokes stirred to remind him that Jack Dansing might wear the cloak of civility now, but beneath his veneer hid a boy who only saw an Indian and not another boy. He crossed his arms, let the thick muscles stand out and widened his stance. If the mayor wanted to get physical, then Jud would take appropriate action. If the mayor wanted to be insulting, then he'd handle that as well.

For a second, Dansing's calm fractured to show the real antipathy beneath the surface. "I warned Vance when you showed up that something was going to happen. Always did when you were around. We all knew who played those pranks back in high school. You just never got caught." He pointed a finger at Jud and snarled. "The sooner you're gone, the better for this town."

Jud saw in this man a typical wanna-be—all mouth and no motion. Jack Dansing was too much a businessman now—too tame—to take action. His moment of hostility vanished as quickly as it appeared. The mayor pulled his dignity around him like a brick wall, sheltering him from a person he found undesirable.

When Jud was a kid, he let people like this make him feel inferior. But he wasn't a kid, and he'd learned that others valued him. Rather than reply and keep the irritation going, Jud remained silent. But he asked for strength: *Great Spirit, guide me to calmer waters. Let the Fathers watch over me. Someone wants me as dead as Mathew.*

He refrained from asking the Cherokee Fathers for justice; he feared they might see it as revenge.

~ * ~

"I get to go home tomorrow." Lottie sat in the chair beside the bed. "Ask Nurse Willows for another chair, Jud. You can't stand up all the time." Her dinner lay in eaten disarray on the bedside table in front of

72

her. "I'd offer you a meal, but I just ate it. Wasn't all that spectacular, but I was hungry. Must mean I'm getting well," she joked.

She squinted and let her eyes go up and down, scrutinizing Jud where he still stood at the door. "Something happened. What?" She trusted her instincts. They'd worked for her so far. The table went to one side. She stood then moved over to him. Their gazes met, and she drilled him with laser-like eyes. "Tell me." To soften the demand, she added, "Please." One hand rested on his chest, a position she normally would never assume, but with this man, touching him like that seemed right.

The evening glow coming through the wide window burnished his face with rich copper. His eyes darkened until she could no longer see the irises. Long lashes shielded them so that she couldn't read what he was thinking, hiding from her. And Jud *was* hiding something. She sensed it. Her hand tightened and gathered the least amount of material, an indication that she was more than worried.

Was he thinking about what to tell her? Filtering the truth for her? Reviewing his options?

"Jud!" She wrinkled his shirt and jerked him, though he moved maybe a quarter inch.

His sigh went over her head, ruffling her unkempt hair. "Someone took shots at me this afternoon." He laid his hand on top of hers, but to remove it or draw comfort from it, she wasn't sure.

Her heart set up a hard beat, fear for his safety as real as if one of her students or family were in a shooter's sights. "You're all right?" That was as much as she could get out; her throat seemed to close on its own, restricting air she needed to ask a thousand questions.

"I'm fine. Don't get all excited." He attempted to soothe her as if she were a child.

She jerked her hand from under his and stepped back so fast she rocked back and forth for a few seconds. "Excited!" Grabbing the rail at the end of the bed, she made her way to the side and sat in a huff. "Your mother is down the hallway. In a coma. Involved in a murder, for God's sake." Her voice rose on a note of hysteria. "You almost get killed with gas fumes and now you get shot at. And you tell me not to get excited?" She ran a hand over her face, trying to regain her composure. The idea of this man getting hurt upset her. Must be from listening to Mary talk about when he was a kid. But peering at the past was not Lottie's way. She wanted to secure the future, and right now, Jud Longtree's future seemed a bit dim. "Listen to me. All upset over a man who seems to think he's impervious to bullets. Yeah," she waved her hand at her throat, "like I'm resistant to being strangled." She rubbed the bruised skin. The ache of her injury returned with her vibrant emotions.

"But I wasn't hit, and that makes me wonder why someone even tried to kill me." He moved in beside her and sat, his thigh touching hers.

"You need a bodyguard, Longtree," she muttered, flustered by the heat he generated. Heat that raced up her side to settle in parts of her she didn't want to think of right then. Her fear turned to anger, and she jabbed him in the ribs. "I suppose you never told Vance so he could check out what happened."

Jud sat like stone and spoke as if his mind were a million miles away. "He was close by when it happened. Came running when he heard the shots."

"How many?"

"Three."

"Jesus Christ! And you're sitting here calmly talking about it when I could've heard through the grapevine that you died." She could feel herself winding up, her energy level soaring sky high, the strength of her worry taking her higher and higher. "Don't you care!" she yelled at him. Too charged up to sit any longer, she stood but swayed and would have fallen against the bedside table if Jud hadn't caught her. "Let go!" To her shame, tears welled up and threatened to spill.

"What do you care? I'm just an *Indian*." Jud spoke as if 'Indian' was a cuss word.

"What the hell are you saying? I don't care because of the color of your skin?" She'd heard a few students speak like that before but never an adult. "If I close my eyes, you aren't any color at all," she snapped.

"Then close them and show me you care," and Jud pulled her

between his legs and used both hands to pull her face to him. His lips met hers in a kiss that was at once tender and hot. Dark and demanding. Light and lingering.

How she wound up with her arms around his neck, tucked next to his chest she had no idea. Common sense told her the hospital wasn't the place to indulge one's desires, but for once, Lottie Amberville wasn't listening to common sense. Besides, Jud held her wrapped in both arms, his mouth slanted over hers, tugging her bottom lip, exploring her mouth, his tongue dancing with hers. Oh no. She wasn't about to stop now.

Chapter Five

Because the doctor thought Mary might come out of her coma Monday, Keenan Waverly stayed the day, brought a book and promised to bother no one, including Jud. The older man's interest was far more personal than anyone knew. Jud knew his reasons so had no objections.

On the far side of the bed from Keenan, Jud settled into a lounge chair. He had all day which gave him time to mull over things. Think about why he came home in the first place. Think about the murder. And think about Lottie. Some of the things he thought about were a damn sight more appealing than others.

"Any change?" The day nurse, Annie Chambers, entered, pushing a machine used to record blood pressure and pulse. Annie efficiently settled the stethoscope earpieces and listened to Mary's heart then laid her fingers gently against a wrist, checking for the strength of the pulse. "She's better today. Her vitals are improving. Doctor Latner will be by this afternoon but said to call if she started waking up."

She nodded to both men then left. Jud sat with nothing to do but remember his behavior with Lottie. He had started that kiss. And he had ended it. Pulled away slowly. Almost couldn't force himself away. Then without a word, he'd left. He never did anything impulsive. But that kiss—that sweet, soul-satisfying kiss—was something he couldn't resist.

And damned if Lottie hadn't gotten right into the spirit by embracing him and returning his kiss with one that rocked his socks. His arms had stolen around her with a mind of their own, while her body had clung to his.

Honestly, how he'd had the power to pull back he couldn't say. Where was the logic in getting attached to a woman and then leaving her? Jud tried to analyze his feelings, search his experience for something similar that would guide him when next he met her. But nothing in his background compared to that kiss with Lottie Amberville.

His practical nature tried to assert itself, but by early afternoon, he admitted that he wanted to see her again. Savor her like a wine. Enjoy what she seemed to offer. And then when his time in Bleaker was over and he had to return to duty, he'd walk away. Yeah, that was a plan.

~ * ~

Vance showed up later that afternoon. He sauntered in and nodded toward Mary. "How's she doing?"

"No change yet, but her vitals are better." Jud stood, not willing to remain seated when Theo Vance was around. A yawn caught him by surprise. He twisted one way then the other, working the kinks out of his body, not used to sitting so long.

Though the police chief nodded to Keenan neither man spoke to the other. Keenan, however, mumbled something about finding supper and left. He'd be back, Jud knew.

"Ernest took that bullet to the lab in Spartanburg yesterday. I got a call just now."

His silence might have lulled a weaker man into asking what the call was about, but Jud waited him out. The beep of the heart monitor went on and on before Vance acknowledged he wasn't going to ask.

"Those shots came from a .30-30 rifle that has been fired before around here." Vance put a shoulder to the wall and casually took out the notebook that Jud was beginning to dislike. Too many bad things were recorded there. Vance thumbed through the pages until he got to the one he wanted. He scanned the page then continued as if Jud had asked for more information. "Friend of mine works at the lab, and he remembered the rifle, believe it or not. An old Sears Roebuck Ted Williams lever action Winchester .30-30 rifle. Not many of them around anymore."

For the space of several heartbeats, Jud relived those terrifying days shortly after someone killed—murdered—his father. Three times someone had fired at him. Only once did he recover a bullet, and that's because he was mad. He had run the first two times, but the third time he took cover and waited out the shooter. Then he dug the bullet out of the tree and took it to Police Chief Martin along with a bullet he'd saved from the same gun. A bullet that took down his first deer. His mother had reported the weapon stolen earlier. She still had a copy of the police report in her records at the house. Someone had broken into their home sometime after his father's funeral, tossed around a few things but only took the rifle and ammunition.

As a kid, Jud knew the police chief thought he had the rifle and was looking for revenge. The spent bullet was a dodge to get out of trouble if anyone got hurt. At least that's what the chief told him. Evidently the man had sent the bullet into ballistics in Spartanburg without telling the Longtree family. The rifle was never recovered.

"IBIS—Integrated Ballistic Identification System—got a match. Gave the firearms examiner several suspects, but it was the same rifle Mrs. Longtree reported missing. Registered to your father. Matched that trophy bullet you brought in to Martin and the one that you said someone fired at you when you were a kid."

Imagine his dad's rifle surfacing over twenty years later.

Vance hitched his gun belt higher and scowled, his forehead turning into a virtual ladder of folds. "Why did someone steal that rifle and use it to take pot shots at you when you were a kid? And why bring it out now and try to kill you? I'm assuming whoever it was back then didn't want to kill you. But it sure looks like they do now."

"I agree. At least two of those shots were close enough. If I hadn't moved purely by chance either one of them would've injured me." He remembered the first time his dad took him hunting. He managed to kill a small doe but had a sore shoulder for a week, the rifle kicked like a mule. Could that kick have saved his life this time by throwing the aim off?

"I went back to the cemetery and searched the area again but found nothing new. There's no lead as to who took those shots. If I were you, I'd be careful."

"Not to worry about that. I'm always careful. Nature of my training. But the question is," and Jud turned to face the chief, "why does someone want me dead?"

~ * ~

Jud returned to his mother's home late that night, frustrated by his discussion with the doctor. Mary wasn't awake yet. But Latner wasn't concerned. He assured Jud that comas, even medically induced ones, could be unpredictable. Mary might be out from under the medications controlling her unconsciousness but that didn't guarantee her waking up. Latner urged Jud to get some rest.

Lying in a soft bed didn't help him sleep though. Instead, his mind conjured Lottie. She had come by Mary's room when she checked out. Her demeanor was pleasant, but her eyes told a different story. His unexplained departure had hurt her. "I'm staying with Ashley tonight, but I'm going home tomorrow. I want to sleep in my own bed. The school administration made me take a week off."

She wanted to say something else. Jud could tell. Her uncertain posture, the dreamy expression on her face, told him all. Because his behavior created this hesitancy, he prompted her. "What?" he asked, the softness in his question meant to soothe.

Lottie lingered in the door, her mouth working then let her gaze fall before asking, "Will I see you again?" He noticed that she held her breath, though he would have made a bet she didn't realize it.

He was putting himself in line for heartache if he went to her. Tangling her life with his might not be such a great idea right now, but he could no more ignore her than he could walk away from his mother. But he never rushed into anything so he moved forward cautiously. "How about I bring a tall cup of dark coffee when I show up?" Jud committed to neither a time nor place.

Her countenance cleared, her brow smoothed and that wide smile of hers put to shame even that of the lovely Ashley Johnson. "That would be perfect."

~ * ~

Jud wondered why he was standing outside Lottie Amberville's house the next evening, holding two steaming cups of coffee.

He'd spent the day with his mom and Keenan while friends came and went. Several ladies from the Smokey Mountain Cherokee Council stopped by, being friends of Mary's for years. Ashley and Cooper showed up, as did Lottie. She brought coffee, and they talked over two hours. Before leaving, she made a point to mention that she'd be home that evening.

~ * ~

"Lovely house, but it looks better inside."

Jud, with two steaming cups of coffee in hand, didn't jump, but only because he heard her come up beside him a second before she spoke.

"Were you going to knock?" Lottie held a small bag of milk and cereal. She stood shoulder to shoulder with him, staring at the house rather than him.

"I thought about it." He drew in a deep breath, more to settle his nerves because the scent of her perfume lingered around her and set his body to thrumming. This wasn't how he usually operated. He only interacted with women on a purely physical level. But Lottie was different, appealed to him beyond the corporeal.

She cut her eyes up at him, her face outlined by enough light from a streetlamp so he saw the uncertainty in her expression. Was she afraid he would knock? Or that he wouldn't?

"This is probably not a good idea." He held one of the coffee cups out to her. "No matter what I do, this town thinks I'm a bad influence. Your rep isn't getting any shinier standing here with me."

She took the cup, transferred it and the bag to her other side and took hold of his arm. "My rep is as safe as I want it to be. Besides," she pulled him along with her up the walk until she stopped at the door, "I have a feeling what I hear about you and what I know about you are two different things." She dug a key out of her pocket and unlocked the door. Before he could ask her to explain, she swept up his hand again, led him through the door and kicked it closed. "Now stand right there." She set the cup and bag down on a hall table, took his cup and put it beside hers then moved deep into his personal space. "Did you mean that kiss in the hospital?"

In less than the thump of a heartbeat, Jud acknowledged her directness and accepted the challenge by pushing both hands deep into her thick mane of jet-black hair. His lips answered her. Soft and slow, he used his tongue to outline the edges of her lips before slipping in to taste her honey sweetness. He flowed into her mouth, absorbed her with only the touch of his hands and lips.

A slight sucking sound teased the air as he released her. He went back for one tiny kiss then opened his eyes. Hers were still closed, her breath somewhere this side of heaven, it looked like. Her hands had settled at his waist, her tall statuesque body stretched up on tiptoes, the better to savor what he dished out. Their hands and lips the only points of contact.

Her sigh whispered down his shirtfront as she leaned her forehead against his chest. "Oh my, I think you meant it. I'll have to think about how to improve on that in the future. If that's possible." She pulled back and gave him a soft smile, one that melted his stubborn heart just a little.

He wasn't about to tell her that she couldn't improve on their kisses. They'd have to move on to something new 'in the future'. But for now, he could exist nicely on that kiss and maybe a few more before he left.

Despite how she made him feel—loose and a bit unconventional— he still had doubts about being there. "Lottie, I just came over to check on you."

Her eyes dropped the tiniest bit at the corners, as if he disappointed her. "I'm glad you did. And you brought coffee, too. You're such a lifesaver. I'm addicted to this stuff." She nodded toward the living room. He hesitated as she sat at one end of the sofa, with a wave of her hand to the other end. Apparently, she was trying to keep their contact casual. He knew it was anything but that. However, he'd go along with whatever she had in mind so he followed her into the room.

He perched on the edge of the cushion, uncomfortable now. His mind searched for something to talk about that wouldn't get him deeper with this woman. "Ashley said something about your family and coffee." He sipped the brew, surprised that it was still hot.

"Was there ever a white person married into your family?" Lottie sounded serious.

Jud couldn't see the point to her unexpected question but gave her the only answer he had. "No. Mom is full blood Cherokee. Dad was as well. Their families were from the original tribes in Georgia in the late seventeen hundreds. Her great grandfather several times over was one of those who were relocated from their homes in the south to Oklahoma."

"Ah, yes, the Trail of Tears. Mary and I have talked of family but never of our ancestors. But that, yes."

"Her family—and my dad's—managed to keep the stories of what happened alive, their family history. Both families returned to Georgia. Dad's family then moved to South Carolina. Somewhere along the way, Mom and Dad met, married and I was born. You know the rest, I'm sure." His coffee suddenly tasted as bitter as his words.

"No, actually I don't. Mary often told me about her family—you and Jacob—before her husband died. But she never spoke of the years after. Before you left Bleaker. Somehow though," she turned her cup around and around, avoiding his gaze, "I never got the impression that she was ashamed. Should she have been?" Her southern accent thickened as her voice lowered.

Jud blew out a big breath, his resolve to not look back or forward, for that matter of fact, weakening. "She might have had some concerns early on. I played pranks on almost everyone. I never meant any harm, but it got to be a game—a challenge—to see how far I could go without being caught. The town's folk got to calling me 'that Cherokee kid'. The cops called me a Cherokee brat, too wild for my own good. Though they suspected, no one could pin anything on me. I was careful, left no evidence. Just silly things that drove the cops crazy." He swirled the last bit of coffee around in the cup while his memories lifted the corners of his mouth.

"Was Vance around then?" Lottie scooted nearer, her interest caught.

"He was on the force and was elected chief just before I left. The funny thing was…" Jud stood and wandered around the room, his pacing indicative of how fast his mind was racing. "I stopped playing games in the fall of my junior year. But the pranks continued. The police never caught anyone, though everyone blamed me." He glanced over his shoulder at her. "I admit I took credit early on for some minor things. The rep just blossomed after that."

"So someone continued tagging the town and let you take the blame?"

"Uh huh."

"Wow. I don't suppose you tried to convince anyone you were innocent." Her voice was as rich as her coffee and just as addictive.

"I tried, but no one would listen." When he viciously crumpled the cup into a small wad of waxed cardboard, he realized the anger of years ago still haunted his heart.

"Jud, someone took shots at you and used your father's knife to kill Mathew. And now you say that the pranks continued when you were younger, though you stopped." Her brows drew together, and her eyes opened wide, energy concentrated in her face. "Someone has it in for you, and they're trying to kill you or have Vance put you away. You pissed off someone, big time. But why?"

"I came back. That's all they needed."

"Why did you return?"

"Not my place to tell. That's Mom's job." His heart constricted, the pain he would suffer if she died surging forward to remind him how fragile human life could be. He had to change the subject, steer her away from the purpose of his return though it was the best reason in the world as far as he was concerned.

"What about you, Lottie? Your family? Did you ever have anything to regret?"

"Regret? No, but this might interest you. My name? Amberville." She took a stance before him, hands on hips, defiant for some reason. "Amberville is the name my great-great-great grandfather took when he

83

left the Jamaican coffee plantation where he was born and raised. He was a slave at Amberville Falls. His white father owned the place. That's what I meant about having someone of a different color in your family. Our family is a mixed bag of colors, but Jud," she paused dramatically, "no one ever tried to kill me for the color of my skin."

She wasn't going to let this matter rest, returning to his near-death and the murder of Mathew like a GPS. "You said once that Mathew Jetter was your best friend. Explain that." She drew him back to the sofa, sat and gently tugged his hand until he sat beside her.

Jud heaved a sigh and ran a large hand over his Marine Corp buzzed haircut. "I got to high school and did something stupid in class. I rarely did that. Saved all my games...pranks...for after school." He dropped his eyes, ashamed now of some of his shenanigans. "The teacher sent me to Mathew's office. Meeting him was like..." Jud searched for a word that described walking into that office, seeing the tall man waiting there for him and feeling like he'd found a friend at last."

His voice caught as he noted Lottie motioning him to continue. "We became friends. To avoid playing favorites we were student and principal during school, but at the end of the day, Mom and I would visit him. I spent hours at his farm, working on the place. Taking care of his garden and hay field." Jud leaned forward, his arms resting on his knees, his focus somewhere far back in the past. "No matter that this is such a small town that everyone knows everyone else's business, no one ever knew about us. If there could have been a perfect man to take over after my father's death, Mathew was the one. My grades improved, though I said nothing in class or indicated that life was better."

Shifting so he didn't have to face Lottie, he remembered how it was—that last day. "My grades along with Mathew's letter of recommendation got me into the Marines. When he walked me to the bus the day I left, I wanted to hug him, but several guys were there. Some of those who had made my life hell in school and out. I remember..." He dropped his head, as ashamed now of his action as that morning.

"What?" Lottie slid her hand along his arm until her palm rested in the curve of his, interlocking her fingers with his.

"I pretended to be mad at him. Like he was forcing me to leave. I yelled at him and said some stupid things. Not a lot. But enough so Jack Dansing and the others would think I was tough." His eyes stung, and he turned his head away from her, afraid he'd humiliate himself. Before emotions could run away with him, he ran the back of his hand under his nose and sniffed. "The whole idea was Mathew's, but I wrote a letter to him as soon as I could and apologized. He played along with me at the bus stop that day, as if we really hated each other. He yelled back." Jud smiled for the first time. "*His* first letter to me was an apology!"

"He must have loved you very much." She wrapped his hand in both of hers and leaned against him, sharing her warmth, offering support.

"Yeah, I think he did. I know I've never met a finer man, and I've been around some great examples in the Corp. We wrote back and forth for years. I'd call him, or he'd call me if I was state-side. We tried to meet up somewhere away from Bleaker at least once a year. From the beginning, Mom knew about Mathew's attempts to make a man of me. She admired him as much as I loved him." His throat tightened in a painful spasm. "That's going to make his funeral a tough one tomorrow."

He squeezed her hand but gently disengaged. "I've got to get some clothes ready. But Lottie, would you meet me tomorrow after the service so we can put our heads together? See if we can't make sense of his murder?"

"Sure thing, Jud." She followed him to the door and leaned against the frame as he walked onto the porch. "But it's going to feel like a long time before I see you again. I think..." She skipped out the door and up to him, grabbed his shirt front and pulled him down to her, "I need something to hold me until we meet again." Her kiss seared his heart and set his body on fire. Before he could get as involved as her, she scampered back into the house with a giggle and closed the door. The lock clicked in place, and the light went off before his scattered brain could function again or his raging testosterone could settle.

"Well, I'll be damned!"

~ * ~

Lottie left her car on Main Street and walked to the Baptist church. People streamed in the same direction, all focused on saying farewell to a friend. Mathew had served as principal of Bleaker High School for thirty years. Many parents in the community went to school when he was there. As far as she could tell, there were as many young people as adults in the crowd. School was naturally closed for the day. Bleaker was not yet such a large community that the death of a prominent and popular person was taken for granted.

Off to one side of the church's steps stood Walter Vance and Peter Dansing. Once again, they were arguing. Coming to fisticuffs today would be appalling, Lottie thought. They seemed to hiss at each other, back and forth. Peter poked a finger in Walter's chest hard enough to rock the shorter boy back a step. While he rubbed the spot, Peter kept on talking. Perhaps she could help. When teens were upset, they often acted out their sorrows in unacceptable behavior. She suspected this was what she was witnessing.

"Guys, can I help? Is there a problem?" She approached, but wasn't near enough to hear Peter's last words to Walter.

"That's okay, Miss Amberville. Just getting things straight. Leaders and followers. That's what we were debating. History thing, you know." Peter smiled an engaging smile that she knew made the high school girls' hearts flutter. His height complimented a honed physique. Dark hair and dark eyes. She'd never seen him with one particular girl; instead, he dated many. Walter, however, was his constant sidekick.

"Glad you're not about to go into another fight. You guys handling this okay?" She jerked her head toward the church and the funeral about to take place.

"Gonna miss Mr. Jetter. He was a good guy. Did the chief say anything to you about who killed him?" Peter sidled closer and dropped his voice. "That guy Longtree is walking around free. Guess he's not involved?"

"Uh, no. He was freed. A witness cleared him. He was doing something else when Mr. Jetter was killed."

"Really? So when's the big guy leaving?"

"I'd think as soon as his mother's no longer in danger." Lottie thought Peter asked a lot of question for someone his age. However, his father was mayor and his mother held a prominent spot in the town's social circle as well as in the Mothers Sports League for the area so he might be more in touch with the investigation than other students. What did surprise her though was how quiet Walter was. Being the chief's grandson, living with the man, she'd have thought the boy would have had questions.

"Are there any other suspects?" Peter continued with his questions, seemingly unaware how odd his school counselor thought the conversation was. "Is there a motive?"

At that point, Walter thumped his friend on the shoulder. "We gotta go." He looked decidedly uncomfortable, his blond hair and blue eyes attractive, the worry on his face not so much.

Before Lottie could say anything else, offer counseling, a friendly ear or lead the discussion into why Peter was so interested, Julie Dansing stepped out of the church's front door. Her expression darkened a little when she saw the trio. She caught Lottie's eye and nodded but said in a low sweet voice, "Boys, you need to come inside now." Her wavy shoulder length hair framed her face and softened the grief Lottie saw. She always thought of Julie as the epitome of femininity. Fresh faced, sparkling eyes, wide smile and a soft word. The woman exuded comfort.

Julie ushered the boys ahead of her, but Lottie stayed outside.

Seeking some of that comfort the other woman seemed to have found, Lottie touched the necklace that lay against the stark black of her dress. Mary'd had it and matching earrings made for her. The design depicted a jagged line representing mountains, with a flat line beneath representing the prairies. Beneath those lines, tucked into the broad curve of the teardrop-shaped silver pendant was a wavy line, symbolizing a river. Together the lines stood for the land that Mary's people traveled in what history called the Trail of Tears. Mary said that journey made her people strong. Lottie wanted some of that strength in the hour to come.

She held the silver teardrop and rubbed one finger over the lines as she moved to the first step and scanned the street. Her place on the front pew with the faculty assured, she waited to enter last.

Where was Jud? He wouldn't miss Mathew's funeral though memories of his father's would surely rise and threaten to overwhelm him. Then again, being Jud Longtree with all he had apparently endured, she imagined nothing but concern for his mother would overwhelm him. No one else approached so she entered the church amid a low hum of voices.

Surprisingly, an American flag covered the casket. The buzz among the mourners questioned why. More amazing was the arrangement of red, white and blue flowers with a sash across it, bearing the Marine Corp insignia. Lottie's hand itched to see if a card hid among the flowers. Who sent them?

She settled into the pew next to Keenan Waverly. Sadness weighted his shoulders, lined his face. A good man dead and his best friend, Mary, in the hospital in a coma. But she saw a more immediate concern there as well and wondered if he, too, thought of Jud. Did Keenan know how much Mathew had influenced the man they both loved?

Love? That thought brought her up short. She barely knew Jud Longtree, though Mary talked about him all the time when they were alone. Lottie tucked that disturbing thought in the back of her mind; other things demanded her attention now.

The low noise that hummed through the church when she entered settled into a chorus of whispers. Adult male bass notes mingled with the tenor of school boys. The soft undertones of women in the congregation added the all-important alto while the soprano notes came from the girls. Mingled among the chorus of voices were the bell choir notes of the children, adding a sparkling quality to the refrain.

Lottie still concentrated on that unexplained flower arrangement when the conversations around her took on an odd quality and caught her attention. The rustle of bodies in stiff clothes swelled as did the noise then like someone switching off the sound to a movie, a silence descended that was too sudden, too deep. She looked to her left where Mayor Dansing, his wife Julie and son Peter sat in the front row. Beyond them sat Police Chief Theo Vance and his grandson, Walter. Dignitaries from the community sat behind them. Her eyes traveled back along the rows as all heads turned; short gasps echoed in the silence before a tension-filled calm settled.

An inkling of suspicion eased into her heart as her gaze finally made it to the open doorway at the back of the church. Shock left her as dumb as the others.

At the door stood a marine in full dress uniform, dark blue trousers with creases so sharp they looked solid, the red stripe down each pant leg a blaze of blood. The dark blue jacket trimmed in red, belted in white, with white dress hat, complete with snowy gloves. A sword hung at his side, coming to mid-calf. On the shoulder of that long narrow sleeve was the red and gold symbol of his rank. Master Sergeant, Lottie remembered Keenan saying the day they met.

Into the dim golden glow of the church interior shot an unexpected blaze of sunlight, a radiance through the stain glass window over the baptismal pool behind the alter. The light fell down the center aisle and illuminated the marine's face, turning the red-hued skin to copper, setting off the angles of Jud Longtree's solemn face. If Lottie had never believed in heavenly signs before, she believed in that instant.

While Jud stood at attention, Brother Williams mounted the platform steps and took up position in front of a chair, near the altar. As if rehearsed, the minute the pastor stilled, Jud began a slow march down the aisle, each step measured and solemn. Lottie imagined the congregation's collective heartbeat coming into sync with his steps. Up the aisle he came, his face impassive, his hands moving in formal swing. At the head of the aisle, six feet in front of Mathew's coffin, Jud stopped, snapped to rigid attention and in exaggerated slow motion brought up his right hand in a salute. His movements choreographed with flawless timing, he lowered his hand, turned with a snap to his left and mounted the side steps to the dais, opposite Brother Williams.

When the pastor took his seat, the congregation audibly sucked in air as if they had been holding their breath during that interminable march. Jud, however, did not sit. Instead, he moved to the podium and froze. For a full thirty seconds, he remained as still as an oak. Then he removed his dress hat, tucked it under his arm and let his hard gaze scan the crowd. Many squirmed under his glance.

"Mathew Francis Jetter lies beneath a cover of Stars and Stripes as befits a man who served in the military. He loved four things. His God, his country, his wife and his students." Jud's glance scanned the front row, touching first Peter than Walter. "Mathew finished high school and entered the Marine Corp where he served with distinction for ten years. Most of you didn't know that. Perhaps none of you did. He was a private man, never talking about the past, always looking to the future for his young men and women, as he called his students. When he left the Corp, he entered college and married. Marie was the light of his life. They wanted children, but that never happened. Instead, God gave him an entire town of children. In that fashion, he became my mentor and best friend. He was the father figure I so desperately needed, turning a 'Cherokee brat,' using the label the town once called me, into a marine." He stopped and let the significance of that settle in. "Mathew Jetter gave every child in his care the same opportunities. The chance to do right, learn about a higher spirit that loves and cares, and make a future that is better for self and others. Before me sit fine examples of his work." He paused as if what he had to say next might be hard.

"When I left to join the Marines with his recommendation and blessings twenty years ago, Mathew told me to do one thing. Return with honor, he said. That has been my goal." If possible, Jud straightened even more as he removed his cap from under his arm and set it squarely on his head, then lowered both arms to his side. "I stand here today representing the United States Marine Corp, for once a marine always a marine. Mathew has returned with honor to his Heavenly Father." Silent now, he raised his right hand again and froze in a salute, his eyes focused somewhere over the heads of all. When that hand once again laid palm against leg, he did a sharp about face, removed his cap and sat.

Lottie reeled from shock, her vision dimmed with teary fullness. Gone was the prodigal son of Bleaker. Before the town stood a man who had achieved his life goal—he had returned with honor, as his best friend asked.

~ * ~

When Brother Williams finished the final prayer, Lottie couldn't recall a word he said. Her mind still reeled from what Jud had shared with the congregation. Her attention returned to the service when, to no one's surprise, members of the local Boy Scouts came up the aisle to act as pall bearers. Mathew's greatest pride was serving as Scout Master for Bleaker's troop pack. Two senior troop members, Eagle Scouts now, came forward and positioned themselves on each side of the casket. A third Eagle Scout, Bill Wilder, stood at the head of the casket, ready to lead the procession out to the hearse. However, the funeral directors did not wheel the casket to the entrance until Jud came down the steps and stood at the end, acting as an honor guard.

The packed church emptied quickly, and Lottie saw that many who came late had stood quietly outside during the service. She and the assistant principal entered a car along with the mayor and police chief. No one spoke; like her, each seemed deep in thought.

The sheer number of attendees at the graveside service almost overwhelmed her. Quite possibly the entire community had shown up. The perfect weather remained so, the fates' tribute to a good man. By the time she got to a seat in the second row of chairs, the casket was in place. Seven Boy Scouts stood around the bier along with Jud.

A hush fell over the crowd as Brother Williams blessed Mathew Jetter's final resting place. The congregation shared a prayer, and the pastor stepped back. The Boy Scouts snapped to attention as perfectly as Jud had earlier. With an efficiency that Lottie hoped they'd never have to use in such circumstances again, the young men lifted and folded the flag with a precision that would have made any service man proud. When the folded colors rested in the hands of Bill Wilder, the seven accorded their scoutmaster their finest salute. Lottie saw that Jud joined them.

In a day filled with grief, honor and surprise, one more surprise remained.

Eagle Scout Wilder lowered his hand, laid one hand on top of the colors and paused, his sheer presence demanding that Jud look directly at him. When the scout and marine faced each other, Bill stepped out, marched up to Jud and held out his hands, one under and one on top of the colors. For the first time, she saw Jud's composure crack. He wasn't aware this would happen. His head lowered until he could see the boy and hear his words. "With the thanks of a grateful nation, sir."

A shuddering sigh passed through Jud as he accepted the flag. The scout backed up three steps, turned and resumed his place. Then he turned and led his band of young brothers away. At a nod from the pastor, the people began to move away, all aware that one marine still stood at attention, folded flag held securely in his hands.

Lottie hesitated, but Brother Williams shooed her back to the cars with quiet words: "He wants to be the last." Ashley joined her, and together they stood by her car, the assistant principal and others returning in the formal cars. Lottie stepped forward, her heart aching when she saw Jud finally break his formal stance.

"No, Lottie. He needs this time." Ashley held her back, then directed her forcefully to the car. "That man was all Jud had besides his mother. Even now her life could be in danger."

For the space of an hour, Lottie had forgotten. While they laid Mathew to rest, the only person who might identify his killer had yet to wake up. But when she did… If she did…

~ * ~

The flag lay heavy in his grasp. He focused on the tent flap across from him and left his gaze there. But he could hear. With no family to pay their respects to, the town turned to each other, seeking shoulders for comfort and grieving tears of gratitude and loss. If Mathew could get to heaven based on the tears that flowed this day, his soul would fairly float through the Pearly Gates on a river.

Jud tucked the colors under his arm and maintained his solitary vigil as everyone cleared out. In his peripheral vision, he saw Lottie hang back. He understood her desire to stay. She had a tender heart and no doubt recognized his anguish. But this moment was his. He was glad to see her leave.

When everyone cleared away, when even the men appointed to lower the coffin and return the earth to its former state lingered well past the drive, Jud relaxed his formal stance and let his gaze fall on the silver casket. While Mathew himself had prepared basic funeral arrangements years ago, Jud and Brother Williams scripted the service, Williams being a former serviceman. Jud had two purposes for the things he did and said. First, he honored a man worthy of it. Second, he told just enough about his return to let the killer know he would not leave until that person was caught.

Stepping forward, he laid the flag carefully on the coffin then removed his hat. Taking a knee, he laid a hand on the silver trim and bowed his head. At last he could let his emotions go. Not that he would cry or anything.

Jud closed his eyes only to feel something tickle his cheek. His finger wiped across his face, and to his surprise, the glove came away wet. "So be it then." He closed his eyes again. "Father God and the Great Spirit—my mother would say you are one in the same. I'm not sure so I call on you both. Here lies a good man. Carry him to his family and give him peace. Tell those he loved that he was a warrior— both in battle and in the fight for education. He never left a man—or student—behind."

A sob caught him unaware, and for a brief space of time, he mourned as only one could who would miss the love and leadership of such a faithful friend. While the tears still lay fresh on his high cheekbones, he stood, retrieved the flag and his hat and stepped back. But he had one more thing to ask for. "Great Spirits, give me the courage and wisdom to find the killer. My mother might say I seek revenge, but You will recognize the need for justice."

Afraid he might linger too long, Jud walked away, nodding to the three men who moved forward to finish the burial. Only when he reached the gravel drive did he realize he had no way to return to town.

Tires crunched behind him, and Keenan Waverly's truck pulled up. Neither spoke as Jud climbed in and grunted in relief when frigid air conditioning hit him. Fair as the day was, the formal jacket was heavy and hot.

Jud had to find Lottie but realized he'd never told her where to meet him. He blew a heaving sigh out through his lips then grinned. Hell, Bleaker wasn't all that big. He'd find her soon enough.

~ * ~

Then again, one woman could certainly lose herself if she wanted to, no matter how small the town. Jud looked in the library, grocery, hardware store and the diner where Ashley worked the counter. Cooper sat on a stool, eating a grilled cheese sandwich.

"Wow, Jud, you look pretty." The little boy pushed his glasses up on his flat nose and managed to leave a smear of cheese on one lens.

"Cooper, I think you mean he looks handsome. Ladies look pretty." Ashley tried to lean over the wide counter and wipe the mess off, but he turned his head away.

"Ah, Mom. Stop!" He swatted his mother's hand aside.

"Hey, little brother, that's not nice. She's only trying to make you look handsome. Here," Jud delicately slid the glasses off his face, handed them to Ashley who did a fast cleaning job and returned them to Jud.

"Thanks," she whispered as she pulled Cooper's plate back from the edge.

"Here you go, Coop. Good as new. Now keep your fingers off the glass. Okay?" Jud thumped the boy gently on the shoulder but leaned over to Ashley. "Have you seen Lottie? I can't find her anywhere." Frustration colored his words with a harsh note.

"Now where do you think she might be waiting for someone who needs to change his clothes?" Ashley cocked an eyebrow and leaned an elbow on the counter.

Jud rolled his eyes, not willing to play her woman's game of 'guess where Lottie Amberville is'. He needed a direct answer instead of this subterfuge. He fidgeted for a second, rearranging his hat and the flag he'd laid on the counter. Just to be safe, he moved both further away from Cooper and his eating area. "Ashley, please. I'm hot and tired. Where's Lottie?"

Her face softened, and she swiped the clean counter with a damp cloth as if it were sticky. "She's at your house."

He reached over and squeezed her hand, then ruffled Cooper's hair. Ashley blushed, and Cooper swatted his hand away but giggled. "Thanks." Hat on and flag under his arm, he hastened to the door. Just as he shoved it open and stepped out, he heard Ashley call out.

"Lottie said she knows something that might help solve the murder!"

Chapter Six

Lottie clutched her necklace like a lifeline while she waited for Jud to return. He'd have to change. Then they could talk. As she rode back to town with Ashley, she'd remembered something. Something that Mathew told her shortly before his death.

That information alone might help Jud solve the murder. Not that Vance wasn't working on the case, but she knew the tall marine wanted to find the murderer himself.

But the longer she sat in the backyard swing at Mary's place, her willingness to help turned to anger. What was he thinking? Telling everyone about his friendship with Mathew. Practically issuing a challenge to the killer. Find me before I find you! Someone had already tried to kill him. Now he upped the ante and almost guaranteed the killer would strike again. Not that she was certain Mathew's killer was the same person trying to hurt Jud, but her gut instinct said he was.

"About time I found you." Jud came striding around the corner of the house, to stand next to her. At a disadvantage in the swing, she stood but still held on to the necklace for courage. She no sooner drew breath to berate him about his open challenge from the pulpit then he leaned over and gave her a fast but sultry kiss. "Come on in while I change." He turned and went in the back door, leaving it opened, as if she'd follow him blindly.

Clinching her fists, Lottie stomped into the house only to discover that she had no idea where he was. "Jud?"

"In here." His voice led her down a hall to an open door where she stopped so fast her breath caught as well.

Jud in full military dress uniform was handsome, but the same man, barefoot, in nothing but cotton briefs and low riding jeans sucked the air right out of her and set her heart to pounding so hard her chest literally hurt. Other parts of her lower down pulsed as well and ached as badly. In an effort to catch her breath, she sputtered and drew his attention. He faced her square on, then noticed her expression. "Cat got your tongue?" His grin was of the wicked variety. He stepped closer with each word until his chest and hers were less than an inch apart. "Guess so. I'll have to get it back for you." One arm eased around her waist, pulling her into his body, as he fit his hand to the back of her neck and drew her into a kiss that fired her nerve endings and didn't let up.

This time she lifted her arms and ran her hands over his burred head. On its own, her clothed body writhed closer, unable to get next to the heat and desire that radiated from his skin. Against her middle, she welcomed the fire of his erection, its width, length and power capable of carrying her higher than she'd ever been.

Jud backed her to the wall. "Gotta have you, Lottie." He pulled away just enough to see her face. One hand ran through her hair as his thumb brushed the rich cream-colored skin at the side of her eyes. "Can I?"

"Yes," she whispered as her tongue filled his mouth, savored the mint he'd eaten sometime that morning. She reached for the hem of her dress, but his hand got there first. Up came the thin black material until it bunched over one hip. As if he signaled her, she shifted enough for his hand to ease inside her panties—panties that dripped with passion's own sweetness.

Suddenly he held her only by their kiss—both hands scooted up her thighs and pushed her panties down so they fell around her ankles. One step to the left and one to the right and underwear and shoes were history. His hands came up and that dress sailed over her head and landed beyond her sight.

Back against the wall again, she broke loose and trailed hot kisses over his shoulders, down his chest to nipples that stood out so hard they looked like buttons on fields of sculpted muscle. He lifted her head so he could take her mouth again, then gathered her bottom in both hands. One heave and she lay against his middle, her legs opened against him. Leaning back, she dug one hand between them and levered his briefs away from that proud flesh straining to get to her. One sigh and she slipped on to his body as if it were ordained. No struggle, no pain. No waiting. She was juiced, jazzed and just plain ready for him.

She twisted her hips ever so slightly so the nerves would explode sooner. Her hands locked behind his neck. Her body rocked up and down, bobbing on his erection, stimulating nerves that welcomed the friction. They stared each other into a climax that left both panting and pressed against the plaster. But her body still rocked, pulsed and wanted.

"More, Jud." She rubbed against him. The tiny bud hidden at the top of her mound quivered as she pushed her breast up so he could suckle. Mouth full of silk-sheathed nipple and hands full of her rear, he backed up until his legs hit the edge of the bed. He fell backward then twisted so that Lottie was under him. While her eyes begged him to take her again, he shucked his clothes and returned to her. He unfastened her bra and sent it to join her dress wherever it was. Her wiggling ramped up his excitement as he slid over her bare skin, the intimate sound charging her once more. Deftly he slid into her hot body and pounded her flesh with his. She urged him on. "More. More. More!"

Her climax almost ripped her body in two; she soared so high she knew coming down would kill her.

Jud lifted her hips and turned her, pulling her back toward him, her bottom in the air, her face against the cotton quilt. And went after her again, his body flowing into hers, his voice pulling her with him as he surged forward and shot hot liquid.

Like a bar of gold that gradually melts under heat, both sank to the covers, Jud lying on top of Lottie until he realized she could barely breathe. He slid over only far enough to let her gasp gigantic masses of air as his hand soothed her back and massaged the sweet curve of her ass.

"How did…" Lottie had to suck in more air, "that happen?"

"Unexpectedly? By surprise?" Jud lay with his leg hiked across her thighs, his eyes closed. A sigh caught him, gathered from deep within and easing out slowly. His eyes still closed, he thought aloud. "For whatever reason, you might want to name, we made love and it was pretty…"

"Amazing? Wonderful? Exactly what we both wanted?" Lottie added that last just to see what he'd say. She wasn't even sure if this was exactly what *he* wanted, but he had fulfilled every dream she'd ever had about a meaningful relationship. Everyone told her there was a mate for each person. And despite all odds to the contrary, when you met that person, no matter what happened—or not—this person would burn his way into your heart and mind. Blend into your soul so insidiously that you could never part. Not without pain. She was wondering if she might have found that person.

Jud lifted his head and scrubbed a large hand over his face, as if waking from a dream. "Amazing. That would just about describe what we just shared." Unexpectedly he leaned over and kissed her, a quick meeting of lips that left her blood surging all over again. "Unfortunately, I have things to take care of. *We* have things to take care of." He dragged his hand sensuously over her breast as he left the bed. "Nice. We have to do this again," he whispered in a low sexy voice as he waggled his brows up and down. "Right now, it's time for other things." But he leaned over and gave her another quick kiss. "Can't seem to stop that," was his mock apology. She knew it was fake because he grinned with no remorse.

He pulled on his clothes, gathered hers and laid them neatly on the bed. While he took care of business in the bathroom, she rolled over and propped her head on an elbow. Her hand still fingered the tear-shaped necklace.

Her euphoric mood gradually slipped sideways into worry. That did a fast ride into anger so that by the time he returned with a washrag, she was ready to berate him for carelessness. However, chastising Jud for putting himself in harm's way had to wait because he pushed her over and used a wet cloth to gently wash between her thighs. Maybe his intention was to clean her, but his hand slowed as it eased against her mound, setting her body to tingling again.

"Jud…" The way she said his name came out sounding this side of erotic when that was not how she meant to say it. "Jud!" She grasped his hand and stopped him, not shoving it away but laying it to one side. His attention focused on her, she sat up between his arms where he leaned on the bed.

Lottie lowered her voice, but she couldn't soften the anger vibrating in her words. "You set yourself up. You told them everything. The killer will come after you!" The more she talked the less control she had over her emotions, especially in light of their recent activities. "You're not the law!" She grabbed his upper arms and tried to shake some sense into him then pushed him away to get dressed. "How could you do that?"

"Vance might get the killer eventually, but I want him before I leave. I'm not losing my mom like I lost my dad. Murdered! And no one ever brought to justice for it. Mathew deserves better."

"Your dad was murdered?" Lottie emerged from pulling her dress over her head, shock in her voice.

"Right here in Bleaker. He drove a school bus and was a custodian in the elementary school between morning and afternoon runs. One day he didn't come home. The police found him beside his bus outside town. Someone had beaten him to death."

"Oh, Jud. I'm so sorry." She pushed her hair away from her face and watched how he changed from loving back to the stoic man she first met. "And now Mary is in danger." The idea that he put himself there as well raised her ire. She grabbed his arm and shook it. "You have to be careful. Don't take chances. Let the police handle this investigation." Fear for him welled up, threatened to overwhelm her. Fear made her angry when she should have been supportive. Or helpful.

"I'm going out, Lottie. I'm stopping by the hospital then going to the diner to eat. Maybe Ashley will be happy to see me." He sounded bitter, and she understood that she was the one who'd turned the experience of a lifetime into a hostile diatribe. The implication that she was unhappy around him deserved some attention. Unhappy wasn't the word; *terrified for him* better described her feelings. But he might not appreciate hearing that.

"Jud…" She reached out to him, but he had left already. What should she do now? Vance wouldn't put a watch on him; the chief probably appreciated the idea someone was trying to kill Jud. She could stay with him, but he'd avoid her after their confrontation just now. She needed a reason to be with him. Maybe the killer wouldn't come after him if he thought there might be a witness. Reason… reason…reas…

"Holy shit! I forgot!" Grabbing her shoes, she raced out of the house. She *did* have a reason to be with him!

~ * ~

"Good afternoon, Jud." Dr. Latner met him in the hospital hall as they walked in the same direction. "Your mom is doing well. Should be coming 'round soon. Her vitals are stable. She had a severe concussion, but her recovery is proceeding well." The doctor rubbed his nose and cut his eyes over to Jud. "Mary has a hard head. I've played poker with her, Keenan and Amy Grinder for years now. Mary gets her way about a lot of things." The doctor's eyes twinkled. "She'll pull out of this soon enough to go to the Stomp Ground this summer. Because whites can't go there unless invited, she showed us her dance. I think it's beautiful. She said this particular dance was special." He clapped a hand on Jud's shoulder. "You must be very proud of her."

"I am. I'd like to see her dance again. I haven't been around to do that, and I miss it." Jud stopped outside her door and nodded to the security guard posted there. Vance never refused anyone entrance, but the visits were supervised. "Doc, I need to ask a favor. It might complicate things around here, but I want to keep my mom safe." Would the doctor go along with his plan?

"Tell me what you have in mind, Jud."

~ * ~

Lottie caught Jud outside the hospital as he angled across the street to the Blue Ridge Diner.

"I have to talk to you." She scanned the street as if someone were spying on them.

"We don't seem to have much to say to each other, as I recall." Jud kept walking, ignoring her.

She grabbed his arm and jerked him to a stop, only because she caught him by surprise. "This isn't about us. It's about Mathew's murder." She had his total attention now. "I remembered something after the funeral. But I…" Their time at his house earlier—making love…sharing great sex—filled her head and heart with other things. "…forgot. I don't want the town to hear this." She jerked her head toward the school further down the street. "There's a bench under an oak there. We can talk. You can be out in the open…like you want. We can also see if anyone comes near."

By now, she apparently had intrigued Jud enough that he accompanied her without comment. Once settled, she launched into what she'd remembered.

"Mathew called me into his office to discuss unusual student behavior. I told you that. But what I forgot until today was that he showed me a locker. He asked me to stay late after everyone left. Mary was there but working in another part of the building. The locker was badly dinged, in an unused section near the office. Before he undid the lock on it, he said only one other person knew about it. He trusted that person implicitly but never said who it was." Lottie spoke quickly but softly, afraid that Jud might leave. "He had stored some papers in there."

"Who'd they belong to?" He slanted his head sideways to watch her. Focused on her intently, he rested his elbows on his knees as he leaned forward.

"They were notes he'd made. He also brought out a plastic bag with a bottle in it. The bottle wasn't big, but it contained enough steroids he said to beef up the whole school, not to mention every athlete. I asked him where he got the bottle and what the notes were. Mathew said they were proof that drugs—steroids—were being sold and distributed in the high school." Lottie stopped, the fear that washed through her that evening coming back to haunt her now. The light spring wind blowing against her arms sent shivers up her spine.

"Did he have a name? Someone he suspected?" Jud sat straighter now, turning over the facts she'd shared.

She opened her mouth to speak but instead grabbed his hand and plastered a huge smile on her face. Leaning forward, she kissed him lightly. "Don't move away! Smile!"

Used to following orders, he saw the urgency in her glance. Jud moved her hand from her lap to his thigh—high on his thigh. When her expression changed to alarm, he grinned and repeated what she told him, "Don't move. And smile." He gathered her hands in his but kept them anchored against his rock hard leg muscle. "What's up?"

She didn't have to answer. A black and white pulled up to the curb in front of them, and Chief Vance stepped out. What did he want? Nothing good, she knew.

"Evening, folks." He stepped up on the curb and moved across the sidewalk. "Cozy, ain't you?"

"Evening, Chief." She could tell he didn't like seeing them together. Beside her, Jud nodded but remained silent. But his hand squeezed hers tighter.

An odd thought struck her. What if Vance was the one who tried to kill Jud? He certainly wouldn't want her hanging around him.

"Quite a display you put on this morning, Longtree. Some kind of speech, too. Seems there's a lot about you that folks never knew." He hooked his thumbs in his belt and rocked back on his heels. But beneath the low brim of his cap, Lottie saw the man's gaze drill Jud, seeking an excuse to kick him out of town.

"I've lived here all my life. No one ever knew anything about me. Nor did anyone ever try to find out. Now I'm back...with business to take care of."

"You sure that business had nothing to do with Mathew?" Vance eyed Lottie. She scooted the tiniest bit closer to Jud. "Seems you're right cozy with your alibi there, Longtree." He touched the bill of his ball cap as if saying goodbye. "I'll keep that in mind."

His car slid away from the curb though the chief gave them a long speculative glare as he left.

A shiver caught Lottie off guard. "That man is dangerous. Anyone who underestimates him is a fool."

"Am I a fool?"

"With your background? Huh! Hardly!" She complimented him without a second thought, without coming right out and telling him how much she respected him.

When the black and white eased around the corner, Lottie snatched her hand out of his but again only because he wasn't expecting it.

"Testy, aren't you?" Jud's eyes sparkled in the late afternoon sunlight that filtered through the branches. But the teasing faded fast, and his mouth drew into a straight line. "Who did Mathew suspect of selling the 'roids?"

"Walter Vance."

Jud didn't sputter, probably because marines kept their emotions in check. But she saw the shock on his face.

"Seems like we had a lot to talk about after all."

~ * ~

"We need to talk to Walter." Jud paused in the dark hall, making sure Lottie was close behind him.

"I can't believe we're doing this even if it was my idea!"

Jud turned right past the high school office. His training made this easy, but Lottie sneaking around in dark forbidden territory bothered him. His large hand brushed against metal. The lockers began here. The one they sought was at the far end. "We've got to know what Mathew knew. If Walter is involved, then we've got to have our facts straight before going to the police."

"Going to Vance, you mean." Lottie pulled him to a stop. Her fear permeated the air around them. The heat of her hand burned against his skin.

Jud listened for sound but heard nothing. No one disturbed them. Even when school was in session, all personnel were gone well before midnight. Lottie had deactivated the alarm. Bleaker High had no motion sensors. They were safe, considering the circumstances.

This kind of mission was what Jud handled best. Dealing with the local law wasn't something he looked forward to though. But if Mathew's evidence bore out the fact that Theo Vance's grandson was dealing illegal substances, then they had no recourse but to present it to the chief and hope for the best.

Better yet, take the evidence to the Feds. Yeah, that might be the best plan. Jud ran through scenarios and discarded them as they neared the far end of the hall.

"Do you have the combination to this lock?" His gloved hand fondled the lock, but Lottie moved across from him.

"I'll open it."

"No, you won't. I didn't want you here, but you forced your way in. That doesn't mean I'm gonna let you touch anything and get more involved. Now hand over the combination." He held out his hand, but she brushed it aside.

"I can't get any more involved with you and this case than I already am."

From the tone of her voice, Jud could imagine a deep blush covering her mocha skin. They were involved, with each other. His body tingled as if he stood near a massive electrical source, but whether that charge came from Lottie herself or the imminent opening of the locker he didn't know.

"There!" Lottie reached in and pulled out several papers and a zip bag. "This is what Mathew showed me last week." She pulled out a small flashlight, but Jud clamped his hand over hers before she could switch it on.

"Not here! Let's get this stuff back to my house. We've been here too long as it is." He clicked the locker door closed and replaced the padlock.

As they eased their way out of the hall, he repeated, "We need to talk to Walter."

~ * ~

Jud kept his gloves on as he handled the bottle labeled THG. "I've seen this brand. Mathew was right—steroids. I can't pronounce the chemical name, but it's a designer drug. Can't be detected by drug testing like most of the steroids can." Lottie gave him a puzzled look. "Even in the Marine Corp, there are men—and women—who want to 'be the best'. So they usually take this shit as a pill."

"So if it can't be detected in testing, how do you find out someone's using it…besides that person packing on the muscles unexpectedly?"

"Yeah, that's one way, but if you got a shower room full of naked guys and one suddenly looks like he's getting boobs and never had them before then you start wondering. Happened during my basic training. Boobs, acne breakout and what they call 'roid rage. Uncontrollable instant rage that had no provocation."

"Washed out of the Corp?"

"Big time. As well as jail time for use of a controlled substance."

Gloved like him, Lottie scanned the pages they took. "Jud, you're not going to like this." She held out one page.

He scanned it quickly, shock washing over his expression.

"You okay? The color just drained out of your face. Better sit down." Lottie was beside him, pushing him into a chair.

"Mathew suspected something so put Mom on to surveillance." He read aloud, "'If I walk down the hall, into the cafeteria or roam around after school, any illegal drug sales go under the radar. But Mary is invisible. As a custodian, she's seen everywhere, and no one pays attention to her. So she has become my eyes and ears. It paid off. She saw Walter exchanging a bottle like this for money on three separate occasions on school property. I confiscated this bottle from a locker. No one said anything, but Walter was absent several days. Rumor had it someone beat him up. But Vance never said anything so I am left wondering what really happened. This might explain the robberies in the county over the past year. Reports from larger cities say theft has gone up as well. Have to get money somehow to support their habits. Bleaker sure has no way for kids to make that kind of money. Most users are athletes. At least the ones I know of. Student names, dates and places are listed on a separate page.'" Jud searched through the pages until he found the one to which Mathew referred. He nodded and continued reading. "'Mary reports to me each day. Our plan is to watch Walter and see who supplies *him*. We'll meet Saturday morning in my office and compile this information into something we can present to

FBI agents in Atlanta. Walter is not the brains of this operation by any means, but he's a handy dealer. The question is, will the head of this mess be caught as well?'"

Jud slumped, his mind going round and round. "Mom could've been seen while she spied on Walter. Whoever killed Mathew may have tried to kill her as well."

He left the most important part unsaid. But Lottie said it just to make it real. "Someone may still try to kill her." Her hand rested on Jud's shoulder and squeezed in sympathy.

"I always knew that, but this..." He leaned against the table. "I've tried to plan for every contingency in case..."

Lottie moved to the chair next to him. She reached over and clasped his hand. "What can I do to help?"

His shoulders were so tense he hurt. Lottie was afraid; her eyes were wide, her chin quivered the tiniest bit as if she were holding back tears.

"Come here." He pulled her to him and sat her on his lap. Her warmth seeped into him and helped ease the apprehension that wracked him. "We've got to be cautious now. But bottom line, we have to talk to Walter and see if he'll crack. He's related to Theo, but first impression..." Jud snuggled Lottie closer to his chest and relaxed a bit more when her arm snaked around the back of his neck. "When do you go back to work?"

"Next Monday. But I have a tutoring session with Ashley Thursday that we can't ignore. She's got a major test coming up."

"Do what you normally do. Can you get Walter alone somehow?"

Lottie sat on his lap in silence, her gaze unfocused as if searching for some plausible reason to get to Walter. Suddenly she laughed right out loud and snapped her fingers. "Dang, I'd forgotten! Walter is coming to me!" She cut her eyes over at Jud, giving him that sideways glance that begged him to ask her why the boy was coming to her instead of them having to hunt him down.

Jud surprised her with a quick kiss. "Okay, Miss Smarty. How, when and why?"

"Walter does odd jobs. One of them is yard work. I made an

appointment with him to come Saturday to do work in my back yard. Trim away winter dead brush and get the ground ready for some flowers. So he'll be there this weekend. You wait inside until he shows up, and we'll talk to him then."

"You can't get him here any sooner?"

"Well, I don't know." She pulled her brows down until the lines dived between her shapely brows. "I suppose I can call him and see if he can begin tomorrow after school." Lottie leaned her head against Jud's. Then yawned. "I can ask him to come early since I can't return to school yet. I want to work in my garden while I can. How's that?" She reached for the phone, but another yawn almost cracked her jawbone.

"Perfect. But I think you might wait until later to call." Jud set the phone back in its cradle. He pushed her gently off his lap and slipped his hand in hers. "It's almost two in the morning. Time to get some rest." He led her down the hall.

Beside her bed, he stripped her of her shirt and jeans. Then he eased his clothes off. All the while, he grinned like a cat about to savor something tasty.

Lottie's attentive gaze aroused parts of him, and she quipped, "You call this resting?"

~ * ~

"Miss Amberville, this place is a mess." Walter propped a rake and shovel against the wall. He laid a pair of clippers and gloves on the chair beside him. "You should have called me sooner."

"Soon enough and yes, I agree, things are a mess." But Lottie didn't refer to the back yard. She feared Walter would run when he saw Jud. Worse, would he go to his grandfather with some kind of lie about harassment?

"The only way to clean up this mess is to confront it directly." She spoke aloud, but Walter misunderstood.

"Pulling weeds and cutting branches is pretty direct, Miss A." His gelled blond hair laid in a stylish curve over his head. His boyishly handsome face would probably remain the same through old age.

But for the first time she noticed signs of skin eruptions along the edges of the hairline on his forehead. A spot or two along the side of his nose. Acne. His upper arms bulged with muscles she'd not seen there a year ago. Had the boy grown up, or had he illegally acquired the bulk that helped win football games and be a star shot putter on the track team?

With his square jaw and blue eyes, he'd never lack for attention. Sadly, he was about to get the kind of attention he'd rather avoid.

"Come inside, Walter. There's something we need."

Though bright, Walter was naïve. He followed her in the back door and passed her. The snick of the lock sounded sharp in the kitchen. Lottie stood with her back to the door, suddenly afraid of what was coming.

"What's up?" Walter's brows drew together, and his eyes grew suspicious. "You gonna seduce me, Miss A?" His full lips stretched into a grin. "Well, well. What do you know?" He stepped toward her, his every move wily and suggestive.

"I wouldn't do that if I were you." Jud stood at the far side of the room.

"What the hell are you doing here?" Walter apparently imagined a good time for him and the counselor, and now this guy was butting in.

"I need some information." Jud moved into the room but kept the boy between him and Lottie. Her expertise at martial arts would slow the kid down if he made a break past her.

"What kind of information?" Any fear Walter might have experienced turned into contempt. "Does my grandfather know you're here? Talking to me?"

"Is there a law against talking to you?" Jud approached anther foot.

Instantly the boy lost his cool. Anger burned brightly in his words and darkened his face to a dull red. "I'm outta here." Walter shot a hot glare at Lottie. "Open the damn door."

"You're the dealer. Who's your supplier?" Jud got right to the point.

Lottie wanted to roll her eyes in exasperation at how crudely he cut to the chase. Then again, this situation could get out of hand quickly.

Best to get it over as fast as possible.

"I don't know what you're talking about."

"I've got a witness that can place you with three students. Have the times and dates, too. You were exchanging money for steroids. THG to be exact. I bet the bottle I've got probably has your fingerprints all over it. Want to try and talk your way out of that?" Jud got to the point quickly.

"You're lying!" Walter ran a hand through his hair, mussing the sculpted locks. Alarm widened his eyes and raised his voice to the first edge of hysteria.

"Want me to name names and tell you where you met each person?"

Walter said nothing, turned from both and shook his head. He drew into himself, hunched over, bringing his arms closer until he crossed them over his chest. He shot a hostile glare at Jud. "I'm not guilty of what you're saying. So what happens next?" His words were mean, nasty, full of contempt.

"We have proof, Walter. No question about it," Lottie interceded.

A wicked smile of understanding crossed Walter's face, but did nothing to lighten the mood in the room. "You want me to roll over on someone, don't you?" he crooned. "I'm not guilty so there's no one to turn over," he snickered and straightened up.

He thinks he has us despite the evidence we say we have. Lottie had been thinking as Jud and Walter talked. Walter knew his position in the community because of his grandfather. Everyone liked him for himself. An intelligent creative kid, no one hung with him as much as... She caught her breath. No way. But the more she thought about it, the more plausible the idea.

"You'd never give up your supplier, Walter." Lottie hoped Jud would follow her lead. "He's important to you." Walter nodded, but she suspected he did so unconsciously. "And he'd hurt you if you told on him." No response other than his shoulders hunching in a bit and his head dropping ever so slightly. She was on the right track.

"You're going to jail. But you can decide for how long. And..." She stressed the word. "You can decide if you're going to take the fall and let someone else go free. To make the money you've made. While you sit in a jail with other drug dealers. Some a lot older and more street-wise than you." She let that idea stew for a bit.

"My grandfather…" Walter began.

"Won't be able to save your butt. This is going to the FBI." Jud hitched one shoulder and quirked his lips as if he didn't care one way or the other. But he left the impression that the local law wouldn't have a thing to say about what happened to Walter Vance.

"What if we make a deal?"

Lottie wasn't about to breathe easy yet. Walter had seen as many TV lawyer shows as she had. He'd have some idea—even if based on fictional shows—what the law could or couldn't do for him.

Jud caught her glance and shook his head once. His turn. "We can help by saying you worked with us to bring the other dealers to justice. But that's the best we can do." He edged closer to Walter and lowered his voice, making it sound twice as menacing as it did already. "You drag your feet and our cooperation dries up."

Walter glanced over his shoulder again, caught sight of Jud much closer than before and dropped his gaze. His expression oozed guilt. At some point, he must have gone from contempt to resignation. His shoulders slumped, and he stuffed his hands into his jeans pockets. But he wasn't as cowed as Lottie thought.

"I have to think about this."

"Why should I let you go now? You're guilty of selling steroids at school."

"I need to think."

Jud let silence do the trick of scaring the boy then said, "You run, and I'll hunt you down." He let menace fill his words, and Walter shuddered beneath the older man's glare. "You warn your supplier and he runs, I'll get you first then the other one."

"Twenty-four hours. Give me that."

"And what will you be doing during that time?" Lottie wondered if Jud might refuse the request.

"I gotta plan." Now Walter acted scared, his fingers tapping nervously at his side, his body rocking ever so slightly side to side.

He'd tried to bluff his way out of the situation, but now his confidence was gone.

"Tomorrow evening at midnight. I'll have someone with us that can pick up the other person," Jud said.

"The FBI, you mean."

Jud remained quiet. Walter's move now.

Lottie held her breath. This was unreal; drugs and murder in her town.

The tense moment broke when Walter turned to Lottie. "I'll be back at midnight. Trust me." She moved aside without saying a word. He left, closing the door quietly behind him.

Jud pulled out his cell and dialed a number. "He's away from here. Follow him but keep out of sight." Before she could grasp what he was saying, he pushed a button then dialed another number, repeating the same message.

"What the hell are you doing!"

"Eyes and ears. Insurance that the kid doesn't run. I want to know what he's doing every minute that we can watch him. We'll catch a drug dealer, but we might catch a murderer, too." Jud pulled her by the arm and headed for the front door. "We're going to get something to eat."

Lottie dug in her feet and protested loudly. "Wait a damn minute! Who's watching Walter?"

"We are." Jud walked on ahead of her without waiting to see if she was coming or not.

But she ran to join him. "So who else is watching that boy? Who'd you call?"

"Keenan and Ashley."

~ * ~

He refused to meet her glance. But she followed when he walked to the diner. Jud heard her sputtering the entire time. He wanted to smile, but few things about this trip to Bleaker were worth the effort. Lottie Amberville speechless, however, could be considered something to smile about. He was learning to appreciate her unconventional approach to things. Going along with the kid about not wanting to give up his supplier was a stroke of genius. Made her appear more sympathetic. She managed to turn his aggression aside.

As he entered the Blue Ridge Diner, he did a quick recon of the place. Ashley was out somewhere following Walter. Staying safe, he hoped. He recognized several in booths, one of whom was Jack Dansing, the mayor. He wasn't in the mood to talk with the man but did need to be visible. Having Lottie with him helped.

Jack Dansing sat facing the door so saw them enter. He waved them over.

Lottie groaned under her breath, but Jud slipped his hand to the small of her back and guided her to the booth. "Stay focused," he whispered.

"What brings you to Bleaker, Longtree?" Despite the words, Jack spoke in a conversational tone, not as if he begrudged Jud's return. He motioned them to join him. All a political ploy for the watching constituents.

Jud caught Lottie's eyes and held her gaze, attempting to tell her they could use the mayor, pump him for information. And an alibi if necessary. After all, Walter and his son Peter were best friends.

Jud moved aside so Lottie could slide into the booth, then he sat beside her. His arm went over the back of the seat. He wanted Dansing to get the idea they were close. Lord, he was beginning to think like Lottie now, creatively, instead of his usual careful plodding pace.

Dansing nodded to the waitress who brought two more menus and took their drink orders. "Your purpose for being here?" he asked again.

"Mom asked me to come back for a short visit." Jud read the menu, without making eye contact with Jack.

"Not much of a visit with Mathew murdered and your mom unconscious, is it?"

"Not much," Jud agreed.

"Leaving soon?"

"When Mom is well and the murderer is caught."

"Vance doesn't seem to have any leads on the murderer."

Jud said nothing. This game of cat and mouse with Dansing was going nowhere fast so he decided to change the direction of the conversation. "Tell me about Bleaker since I left." He gave his order and Lottie's to the waitress, handed over the menus, then sat back to wait for an answer.

Dansing humphed as if he couldn't believe Jud would ask for a recap of the last twenty years. "In a nutshell?"

Jud nodded and slipped a hand to Lottie's shoulder, more to keep her quiet and calm. He sensed tension like a coiled snake next to him.

"Well," Dansing ran a finger through a water ring on the table then caught and held Jud's attention. "Some of us got married and had kids." He motioned to himself. "Some of us left and did other things." He waved a hand to Jud. "Some moved in," his hand gestured to Lottie, "and others moved out. Kids grew up and did what we did as kids."

Jud couldn't help the snort that came unexpectedly. "No one did what I did as a kid."

"True, I bet. Some got more power." All three knew he meant Theo Vance. "Some grew weaker. The town itself has grown little. Bleaker's pretty much like you left it."

"So perhaps the person who killed my dad still lives here. The person who murdered Mathew is still here. Whoever tried to kill me is still here." By Jack's reaction, that last bit was news.

"Someone tried to kill you?"

"When I was a kid and again right after I returned a few days ago."

For some reason, that seemed to bother Jack, but Jud couldn't figure out why.

"Why would anyone want to kill *you*?" Jack probably emphasized 'you' in order to make Jud feel unimportant.

"No idea. Guess someone just doesn't like me."

The three fell silent as the waitress laid out their food.

"Your boy and Walter Vance seem to be good friends, despite the fight they had Saturday morning."

"Walter's parents died ten years ago, and he moved in with Theo and Janice. But then Janice died of cancer, and that left Theo and the boy. Vance took her death hard and for a while almost forgot Walter. He and Peter hooked up, and they're thick as thieves now." Dansing grinned and returned to his steak, potatoes and white gravy.

Thick as thieves. The expression suddenly took on new meaning for Jud. He shot a glance to Lottie who was waiting. Though she said nothing, she nodded at his inquiring glance.

So that's the way it is, huh, Jud thought. She's already thought of that. What if Peter and Walter... He raised one eyebrow in question, and she nodded cautiously.

Chapter Seven

"Let's sit here for a while." Jud patted a place next to him on the wooden bench outside the hardware store. The sun had set while they dined with Jack Dansing. The breeze that warmed the day early on had turned cool. "We can enjoy the evening."

"Yeah, and watch what's going on." Lottie sank beside him and gave him a cheerful grin. One belied by the haunted look in her eyes.

He regretted putting her through this. She lived and worked here and probably planned on being here for years to come. In he came and life as she knew it quickly fell apart. Her hand rested easily in his when he captured it.

"I'm sorry about everything that's happened to you, Lottie."

"Not everything's turned out badly." She squeezed his hand and bumped his shoulder with hers. "One or two things have been pretty spectacular."

"I can think of one, but two?"

"Kisses, Jud. Kisses. And a few other fabulous happenings."

To his great surprise and pleasure, she reached up, laid a hand against his jaw and turned his head to her. Leaning in, she pressed her upper body against his as her kiss overwhelmed him. When she pulled back, he followed her. She gave him another kiss—this one short and sweet—before leaning back and sighing in what sounded like happiness.

"Yeah, two good things," Jud stammered in agreement.

~ * ~

Jud slipped into the bedroom without waking her. He'd been busy, and lack of sleep was catching up with him. Too many things to think about. She wouldn't like what he'd done, but she'd deal. With time, Lottie had focused more on the problems they faced rather than let her creative mind imagine concerns where none existed.

He snuggled next to her, kissed the top of her head and admitted that her creative streak was wearing off on him. His smile faded slowly. His thoughts turned to Walter Vance.

Would Walter turn over evidence against his partner? Would he keep his mouth shut? The more Jud thought about it, the more worried he became. What if the kid talked to the supplier?

Dawn eased over the pines. Light brightened the yard outside the window, and Jud was still awake. He'd given Walter twenty-four hours, and he'd stick by that. But nothing said he and Lottie couldn't keep an eye on the kid in the meantime.

~ * ~

"Have you seen Walter?" Wearing crisp camo fatigues, Jud sat beside Lottie in a booth at the Blue Ridge Diner. Ashley shook her head and looked grim. "Keenan did surveillance early this morning. But he has to work today. Like me."

"Mama, can I have more milk?" Cooper sat across the booth from Jud, wearing a white milk mustache.

"Sure, honey. But be ready to go when Miss Katie comes to pick you up."

"I hope Walter does the right thing," Lottie whispered to Ashley.

"I seed Walter." Cooper wiped the milk off his upper lip with the back of his hand.

"Oh, really? Did you see him this morning?" Jud leaned closer. Cooper talked loudly most of the time.

"Him and Peter were fighting."

"Again!" Lottie threw up her hands in frustration.

Jud exercised a bit more patience. "Were they hitting each other or just shouting?"

"Shouting! Loud!"

"Where?"

"I seed 'em outside when Mama and me comed here."

"Where did they go? Did you see?"

"They walked down the sidewalk then cross the street." He pointed toward the far end of town where the high school was.

"Maybe they were going to school," Lottie speculated.

Cooper's serious expression lightened suddenly. Jud looked over his shoulder to see an older woman and little boy approaching the booth. Cooper began scrambling out of the booth. Ashley put a hand on his shoulder to slow him down and help him get his balance.

"Morning, Katie. Cooper's more than ready to go with you." Ashley kissed her son and handed him off to the babysitter.

"Lottie, can you call the school and see if Walter is there today?" Jud knew of no other way to ensure the kid was somewhere safe.

"Better to ask the other way around. No need pointing out Walter. There would be too many questions. I'll ask who's absent today."

"You're a smart woman, Amberville." Jud bumped her with his shoulder.

"Good grief. You two are so sweet it's giving me a sugar high." Ashley rolled her eyes and left, but she grinned as she turned the end of the counter.

"I have an idea. If Walter is in school, then he'll be there until three. We really need to be out and visible then. But until then..." Lottie waggled her eyebrows up and down. "We can get to know each other better," she whispered.

"Humm," Jud straightened his face and gave her a flat look. "I have to write up a report for the Feds," he began. Then he relaxed his face and let her to see his desire. "But I'll make time for exploration."

"Oh, you!"

~ * ~

"Come get me."

The boy was whispering. Jud could barely hear Walter on his cell. "Where are you?"

"Outside of town, just past the high school. I'm in the woods. When I see Miss Amberville's car pull over on the shoulder, I'll duck in the back seat. Okay?"

Walter sounded scared. Jud couldn't blame him. If he was turning state's evidence, then his life was in danger. An almost tangible fear shadowed his words.

"We'll be there in a few minutes."

Lottie paced, a bundle of uneasy energy.

Tension wound Jud tight, but he could handle the pressure. This was not a mission into the Iraqi countryside. This was a mission to save a small town from drugs. A sideline to finding a murderer, true, but just as important. He needed Walter to get past his fears and feel secure with Lottie and him.

He had already talked to an agent in the FBI office in Atlanta. The Feds would come in as soon as Jud and Lottie picked up Walter and got him safely to her house.

The plan was far from perfect, but the best they had.

Lottie secured the house and slid into the passenger seat. "I hope this works."

Jud eased the car away from the curb. Night's deep black covered their drive along the back streets. Lottie pointed to a stand of thick oaks less than a half mile past the high school, well away from town. Jud pulled over on to the shoulder of the road and hit the Unlock button for the back door.

Someone streaked out of the underbrush and made a dive for the door. Walter threw himself into the back seat and lay flat, breathing in hard gasps.

Jud pulled the car back on the road. He glanced in the rearview mirror but couldn't see Walter. "You okay?"

"Yeah...just...a...bit...winded." Walter sounded like the kid who'd found Mathew's body. Scared shitless.

"We'll head back to Lottie's house and talk there. If you tell us what we need, then we're taking a road trip."

"Road...trip! I can't...leave...town!" Walter's breathiness emphasized his terror. "My granddad...will...kill me!"

"He loves you, Walter. He won't hurt you. He'll understand. But others might not. We have to get you out of Bleaker and somewhere safe." Lottie tried to reassure Walter that everything would be all right. But would they?

Jud pushed the gas pedal a bit harder, a sense of danger making his skin crawl. He heeded warnings; those signs had saved his life more than once during his overseas tours. Beside him, Lottie reached over for his hand. He glanced at her sideways long enough to see that she'd gone pale and was panting.

"Breathe, baby. Breathe." Like her assurance to Walter, his did nothing to improve the situation.

They pulled up to her wood frame older home, last one on a street headed out of town. Jud killed the engine and lights. The neighbors' homes were dark, the time well after midnight. The porch security light was off so no one would see them entering with Walter.

Before Jud could say anything, Walter stuck out a hand. "Give me the key. I want to get inside fast." Lottie handed it over, and he threw open the back door. He scooted out of the car and dashed across the lawn as Jud and Lottie hastily exited the car.

That niggling warning hit Jud like a brick. Something was wrong. He scanned the lawn and house. Nothing he could see. But there was danger.

"Wait!" he shouted as Walter vaulted up the steps and landed quietly on the front porch. He pulled the screen back, stuck the key in the lock and turned…

The night sky lit up like a million Roman candles going off at the same time. The blast's concussion threw Jud and Lottie back against the car. Lottie went down in a heap beneath the wheels. Jud landed hard on his side against the curb. Debris flew through the air and fell like deadly snow. Burning timbers. Scorched metal. Shards of glass.

Jud painfully pulled his body over Lottie. A board hit his back, the impact unexpected and agonizing. He brushed embers off his head, the heat singeing his hands. A sliver of glass wedged in the door right above Lottie's head. His ears rang from the explosion.

Explosion! Walter! Dear God! Did the boy survive?

Beneath him, Lottie stirred and groaned. "Jud? You…okay?"

"Yeah, but…" No way could he say what he was thinking.

"Walter?" Lottie started to yell for the boy, but Jud put his hand over her mouth.

Walter Vance was probably dead, killed in an explosion. A coincidence? He doubted it. The three of them could have easily been standing on that porch when the blast went off instead of just Walter. The last thing Jud remembered was the boy sliding the key into the lock.

Sirens blared as two fire engines rounded the corner. Neighbors poured out of nearby houses, running toward them. Two police cars careened around the opposite corner.

Holy Hell! How were they going to tell Theo Vance that his only grandchild was dead? Murdered!

Murdered! The blast was no accident.

Lottie stood but wobbled so Jud pushed her back against the car. He wasn't steady either and put out a hand for support. In front of them, her house—what was left of it—burned furiously. An elderly woman ran her arm around Lottie and hugged her, soothing her with meaningless but well-intended words of support. A young man approached Jud. "You okay?" He nodded, his gaze focused on the burning house. Maybe the explosion threw Walter away from the inferno. He took a step forward but stumbled. The man held his arm, steadied him.

Small things intruded on his consciousness. His side hurt…probably bruised or busted ribs. His ears still rang; loud buzzing that muted the clang, clatter, popping and crashing sounds around them. His back hurt, and his eyes ran. Tears covered his cheeks. He shot a glance at Lottie long enough to see her crying in the arms of the other woman. She knew.

"You guys all right?" A fireman approached, his turnout gear covered with soot.

How to tell them? How to? Where was Vance when you need him? Not that Jud wanted to talk to him, but there was no recourse.

"We'll live, but…" He swallowed. "A boy was at the door when the house blew. We need to find him."

The fireman nodded and set off in a run for the front of the house. Jud saw him speak to first one then another fireman. One passed off his hose to a third, and the three began going through wreckage. Jud followed. Each step was agony. As much as his body hurt though, his heart hurt more.

Out of the corner of his eye, he saw Vance and one of his officers. Clyde Bell, he remembered. The firemen suddenly clustered around a pile of smoldering boards. The remains of the front door, it looked like.

He stopped, sick at heart. The way the men were acting, the boy didn't need a hospital. He'd go straight to the funeral home. Jud bent over, his hands on his knees and retched.

"Walter!" Lottie screamed. Jud turned to see her running toward the firemen. He managed to reach out and grab her. She collapsed in his embrace, weeping. "Walter," she sobbed repeatedly.

"Walter?" Theo Vance came up behind them. In the light of the fast burning fire, his face paled, the skin taut, his eyes dazed, filled with terror. "He went out an hour ago. Said he had to see someone." Vance turned toward the house. At sight of the firemen and hearing Lottie's words, his mind must have put the evidence together. "Walter!" He broke into a sprint, headed to the one place he didn't need to go.

Lottie gasped. Jud released her and dashed after Vance. He tackled the man and carried him to the sodden grass.

But the old man struggled, clawed the ground even with Jud's weight on his back. One hand out, reaching for what he could never have again. "Walter!" His screams tore Jud apart. He wrapped the older man in a bear hug and held him, held him as sobs filled the night.

"I'm sorry, I'm sorry," Jud whispered repeatedly, Vance unhearing in his despair. They stayed locked like that as firemen carried the body away from the fire and put it on a gurney. When Lew the EMT pulled a sheet over the remains, Theo Vance collapsed, the fight gone out of him for the first time that Jud could remember.

~ * ~

"The evidence is gone," Lottie said in a low undertone. Jud still sat on the stretcher where the doctor had just finished wrapping his ribs. She wore a few bandages herself. Like him, she refused to stay overnight for observation.

"No, it's not."

"The fire destroyed it all."

"Those papers and the bottle weren't at the house."

She couldn't have heard him correctly. The evidence was in a drawer in the bedroom where they slept. True, she hadn't checked on it that morning, but who would have moved it? A chill ran cold fingers down her spine.

"Where's the evidence?" Her words were low and threatening.

"Back where we found it." He could see anger burning in her eyes. "I returned everything last night."

"And you didn't tell me?" She breathed through her nose, disappointment and rage hitting her hard. He didn't trust her. "You decided to do this on your own?" All the passion she expressed in loving him came to the surface, this time directed at his lack of faith in her. She pushed away from the stretcher, shoving it a foot away. "If you're so good at making decisions, then you figure all this out...by yourself." Her tennis shoes squished a rubbery sound as she walked with exaggerated care out of the curtained space and into the ER waiting room.

She drew up short when she saw the people there. Ashley and Cooper sat in a corner, Cooper asleep in her arms. Keenan Waverly sat next to her, her head leaning on his shoulder, her eyes at half-mast. Teachers, firefighters, businessmen, the Baptist preacher. Jack and Julie Dansing stood together near the double door, his arm around her. The only ones not there that should have been were Theo Vance and Walter's best friend, Peter Dansing.

Theo had collapsed at the fire and been admitted to the hospital. He was currently sedated in a room down the hall from Mary Longtree.

Lottie headed for Jack and Julie.

"You all right?" Jack asked as she approached.

"I'll be fine. Where's Peter?"

"He was in Spartanburg, headed home. I called him but just said there'd been an accident. Walter was hurt. I didn't want him speeding to get here and maybe hurt himself." Jack realized what he said and clamped his mouth tight.

"Walter was like a son. He practically lived at our house most of the time. Especially since Theo's been working so hard on this murder investigation." Julie's cheeks were wet from tears that still flowed. "I can't...I...can't..." She turned into her husband's embrace and sobbed quietly.

The sound of feet pounding down the hall interrupted the scene.

"Where's Walter?" Peter ran into the waiting room so fast that his jacket flew out behind him. "Is he okay? How bad is he hurt?" When he saw his dad, he ran up to him and grabbed him by the arm, shaking him like a terrier does a rat. "Where's Walter, Dad?"

But his father couldn't answer. The words appeared trapped in his chest somewhere.

"Mom?" Peter noticed the way his parents and the others in the room were acting.

He saw Lottie and moved to her. "What happened?" Tears flowed over his long dark lashes. She pulled him into her arms and hugged him tightly. Leaning close, she whispered, "He's gone, Peter. He died in an explosion."

Peter buried his face in the crook of her neck and bawled. Jack and Julie hurried over and hugged both of them. Crying filled the silence of the small waiting room.

"What happened?" Peter spoke into Lottie's shoulder. He held her as if she were a lifeline.

How to answer him without giving away what Walter was doing, she wondered. "Walter came to Jud and me with some information he thought was important. We drove to my house to discuss what he had. Walter hurried to unlock the door ahead of us. When he turned the key, it must have triggered something. Perhaps gas fumes or..." She honestly had no idea what caused the explosion. But like Jud, she knew it was no accident.

"Walter died…for that!" Peter backed up, bumped into his dad and tried to keep backing. For some reason, he seemed furious that his best friend died in such a manner. He threw his arms out, knocking Jack away. In a fury, he pointed a finger at Lottie. Wrath filled each word he shouted. "Walter was killed! Murdered! By you and that Indian!" His accusations grew louder and louder, drawing nurses and other staff from the back.

Dr. Hooker, head of ER, stuck his head out. "Lottie, need some help?"

She waved him off though he came on into the room. "I think it'll be okay."

But Peter was ranting now, shouting accusations about her and Jud. Hooker moved forward, but Julie grabbed her son by the shoulders and turned him so he could focus only on her. "Peter, let's go home. We'll talk there."

"He's dead, Mom. Why?" In an unexpected turn around, Peter sounded helpless in light of his recent explosion. "He didn't have to. He didn't have to."

Jack and Julie led their son away, his litany growing fainter and fainter in the softness of forgiving night.

~ * ~

Jud's sigh came at a great cost, his personal reserve of emotional strength gone. Lottie no longer trusted him. His mom was still unconscious, still in danger. Theo was an emotional wreck and sedated because of it. Young Walter Vance was dead. And he was no closer to solving the steroid problem or murder.

He stood in the door of the waiting room and watched Lottie mingle with the people who sat there, silent tributes to the boy and his grandfather. Perhaps concerned for her as well. Certainly, none of them came to check on him. Perhaps Ashley, Cooper and Keenan came for his sake, he admitted.

Walter knew the next person up the drug chain. His death closed that door. The supplier apparently found out what the boy had planned and eliminated him. Seemed murder, drugs and intrigue were not limited to big towns, novels and the movies after all.

Helplessness wasn't something Jud experienced often. Any clue to Walter's death went up in flames at Lottie's house. Any information about the murder was locked in Theo's head; his officers would not release that to him. The only possibility was his mother. When she woke, she'd be able to tell them what happened to Mathew. And she'd be able to tell them about the drug problem. A problem now attached to a murder.

With Theo out of commission, Officer Clyde Bell motioned Jud back into the ER cubicle. Answering the officer's questions would be tricky. Jud had to be as truthful as possible. Lies demanded more lies to continue.

"Why was Walter at Lottie Amberville's house?" Clyde had a notepad out and pen ready. His eyes were red like everyone else's.

"Walter had information about a possible drug problem at Bleaker High School."

"Drugs? In our town?" Clyde sounded skeptical. "Why didn't he tell the pol... Never mind. Continue."

"He talked to Lottie and me yesterday when he was doing yard work at her house. He said he needed time to get some intel together. He'd meet us tonight." Jud had no idea what time it was. "We were going to pick him up, talk through what he knew then possibly drive to Atlanta and turn over the evidence."

"Walter was turning state's evidence against a drug dealer? You were taking him to the FBI?"

The officer was sharp. He put two and two together and came up with the correct answer. And the implications of the police chief's grandson being involved with drugs. "Was Walter a user?"

"Probably, but can't be sure. He did sell though. We have proof of that. However, he was not the supplier. That's who he was going to roll over on."

"Any idea who that might be?" Clyde's pen made furious scratching sounds as it moved across the page.

"None."

"This is quite a story. I'll ask you to stay here. I still have to question Lottie." The click of his pen and the snap of his notepad closing signaled the end of their interview. "I'll be back as soon as I can." But before he left, he turned sad eyes on Jud. "This is gonna kill the chief."

Chapter Eight

Officer Bell said Jud could stay with his mom rather than go home alone.

Jud was surprised to see no guard at his mom's door. Now that he thought about it, he remembered seeing Curtis in the waiting room. Not that he could blame the man for offering support, but he had a job to do, damn it.

He pushed the door open and stopped.

Julie Dansing turned startled eyes at him and froze where she stood on the far side of the bed. Her fashionable purse lay on the sheet. Her colorful shawl draped her lower arm and hand.

"What are you doing here? I thought you left with your husband and son." His surprise rapidly turned to suspicion. Trained to assess any emergency, he watched the woman's expression change from surprised alarm to a calculating calm.

"What do the doctors say about your mother's chances of recovery?" She spoke in a conversational tone, as if they discussed the weather. She ignored his questions.

"She'll wake up any time now." He stepped into the room and let the door swish silently closed behind him.

"That's too bad. We just can't let that happen, now can we?" Julie cut her eyes coquettishly over at him. Her smile made him sick; the curve of her beautiful lips revealed cruelty. One hand eased her shawl back.

A needle was already stuck into the IV injection port in the back of

Mary's hand. But the plunger wasn't down yet. There was still time.

For a woman about to commit murder, she seemed secure in the knowledge she'd get away from him.

"You can't do that and get away." Jud stated the obvious and stepped forward.

"Uh uh uh," Julie warned. "Tsk, tsk. You come closer, Mary dies. Simple as that." She turned a sad face to the woman in the bed. "But then again, Mary's going to die anyway."

"Stop!" Jud held out a hand, his heart pounding hard against the bandage wrapped around his ribs. "Why my mom? What's she done?" Play it innocent; force her hand.

"I'm not one to tell all I know unlike those fools in the movies." Julie tossed her glossy brown hair over one shoulder and preened, obviously comfortable in her abilities. "Let's just say Mary Longtree knows too much about a lot of things." Her thumb twitched.

"Wait!" Jud broke out into a sweat. His mouth went dry. His brain worked overtime to keep his mom alive. He wasn't worried about himself. Yet. Julie Dansing would have to get past him to leave. He'd figure out something.

"I can see those gears grinding in your head. After I kill Mary, you think you can keep me here." When he started to speak, Julie shushed him. "Sorry, but that's not how it works."

"You can't get away with murder."

His words made her laugh. "Of course I can. I've done it twice now. Almost five times. Well, to be honest, I can't take entire credit for the first time. I just watched. That was my darling husband's doing." She chuckled as if the memory was delicious. "He used a baseball bat. Still has the stupid thing."

The color drained out of Jud's face. His skin felt hot and pale. A bat. "He beat someone."

"Oh, yes. Quite efficiently, too. All that baseball practice paid off when he was a kid." Her words were dreamy. As if she told a love story.

"Jack killed my dad." The words came out flat, unemotional. After all the years, Jud never figured to solve that particular murder.

"Old man Longtree threw Jack off the bus that day. Jack gave him hell all the time. Hated that old man. Jack cut through the woods and caught him at the stop sign way out on Linger Road. He threw a rock and hit the windshield. Longtree got off and came after him. Jack beat the shit out of him."

Despite her earlier assertion that she wasn't one to give away information, Julie Dansing was telling more than she probably planned to. Her pride in telling Jud the tale of his father's death was beyond horrifying.

Her words made him sick. He remembered his father as a kind man. His mom never let him see Jacob after they found him so he never knew how badly disfigured he was.

"When you go to prison for murder, Jack will join you."

"Think so?" She shrugged. "I seriously doubt it." She wiggled her hand, enough to make Jud catch his breath.

He didn't know what was in the injection, but it would be lethal. Before the end, she had to tell him who she killed, say it aloud.

"You stole that knife from my mom. Snuck up behind Mathew. Or did you push him against the bleacher and then stab him? You went looking for Mom," he guessed.

Her smug expression told him he got the part about Mathew right.

"You didn't know Mom was there, did you?" he guessed. He crossed his arms over his chest and grinned. "Must have scared the hell out of you when you heard she was in the school at the same time as Mathew. So you think Mom may have seen you kill him, and you have to get rid of her." He nodded, hopefully appearing impressed. "But that's only one murder. You said you killed twice. Or did I hear wrong?"

Full of visible self-confidence that she had the situation under control, Julie seemed to enjoy their conversation. "You can add that whining bastard Walter Vance to the list. You and Lottie scared him badly. He came whimpering to Peter about turning themselves in. I overheard them. When you left to get him, I set an explosive to the door lock. Never know what kind of skills you can learn when dealing with low lifes. And the Internet is just *full* of deadly information.

Almost got that bitch Amberville, too, but that nigger busted up my party that day." Julia gave a snort of contempt at what she probably considered an inconvenience.

"It must have been you who took pot shots at me and tried to gas me to death." His anger threatened to blossom. The woman was mad! Completely over the edge!

"You ducked too fast. And your dad's old rifle is heavy. Kicks like a mule, too. Jack stole that rifle after your old man's funeral. He got a thrill out of you whining about that robbery. Of course, Jack's a bit dense. He never asks questions when I visit other towns. Never asks where I get money to do my social work. Pays, you know, to be acquainted with men in…let's say, the black market." She straightened and tossed her hair over her shoulder, a proud woman listing her accomplishments. "As for killing you with that leaky gas stove, I didn't hit you hard enough. A rather impromptu plan, I admit," Julie Dansing said as she studied her fingernails, her attitude suggesting she saw nothing wrong with murdering someone. "I might have succeeded. Sadly, for our community, you would have died when your home caught fire," she sneered. "I'm not sure what to do with you the next time."

"Who says you'll get a next time?" He straightened and braced his feet wide then fisted his hands at his side.

"My, my. What a show. And all too late." Her hand slid into the purse and pulled out a gun. An ugly Ruger .45. "Not exactly a lady's gun," she cut hard, dark eyes at him, "But then I'm not a lady." She raised her arm and pointed the gun at him in a steady hand. "I'm capable of killing Mary and you at the same time."

A knock on the door interrupted the tense moment. "Jud, can I see Miss Mary?"

Jud's plans went south in a heartbeat. Cooper stood outside, and he sounded determined to come in. Where the hell was Ashley? And Lottie? *Great Spirit, keep them away. I can keep the boy safe, but not all of them. Give me courage, Fathers. Give me wisdom.*

"Invite him in, Jud." Julie's sweet voice belied the devil that drove her.

He moved to the door and reluctantly opened it, pulling Cooper into the room.

"Hi, Jud. Can I see Miss Mary? Mama is talking to Miss Lottie." Cooper pushed his glasses further up his nose and completely ignored the mayor's wife.

"Jud, stay there. Come over here, little boy. Mary is sleeping. You can give her a kiss. I'll hold you while you lean over."

Cooper walked to Julie, unaware of her intentions. He stood in front of her, his arms up, waiting for her to lift him.

"Humm, seems we have a problem here. My hands are full. I'll have to get rid of something in order to hold him." Her thumb moved too fast for Jud to stop. The plunger went down, and clear fluid flooded the IV port.

"NO!" Jud lunged for Julie, but she dropped to her knee and placed the gun to Cooper's head, stopping Jud in his tracks. "Mom! You killed her! You murderer!" he lunged again, but she jammed the gun barrel against Cooper's temple so hard he cried out.

"Killing gets easier with practice, don't you know. Mathew. Walter. Poor thing wanted my son to go with him. Talk to you and Lottie. Something about turning himself in for supplying steroids. The 'roids I brought for Peter to sell." Julie snorted as she lifted Cooper in one arm, the gun now pressed against his tiny chest.

"Am I in trouble, Jud?" Cooper asked in a worried voice.

"No, little brother. You're doing fine. But do what this lady says. Okay?"

"Okay. Are you going to do what she says, too?" His innocent question hurt Jud's heart. So little and fragile, with that monster holding him and a gun half his size near his heart.

"Yeah, Cooper, I'm going to do what Mrs. Dansing says. For a while anyway," he added, shooting daggers of hate at her.

"Good boy!" Whether she referred to him or Cooper, he didn't know.

"Now, Jud, you're going to lead us out of here. The nearest door is to the right. The nurse at the station won't see us. My car is outside that door. Cooper and I," she squeezed him affectionately, "are going for a drive. A long drive all by ourselves. And you won't come after us, or this little man will have an accident."

Her smug attitude scared Jud to death but gave him hope that she might over play her hand.

"Back up, and open the door. Check the hallway. See if it's clear." She motioned him on with her head.

Jud eased the door open, saw no one in the hall and stepped out.

"Hold the door for us."

He stepped to one side and held it open as Julie and Cooper moved into the hall next to the wall. She wasn't taking any chances of someone slipping up on her.

"Now before anyone shows up, we're going to walk quickly to the door. You first." Even now, she held the gun steady and level under her shawl, right at Cooper's head.

Options were getting slim, Jud thought. *If she takes Cooper away chances are she'll kill him anyway.* He needed a diversion. *Cherokee Fathers, help.*

Ten feet from the exit. Five feet. A door opened behind them with a crack loud enough to fill the wide hall.

"Julie! Stop!" Lottie stepped out of the women's bathroom, drawing the woman's attention. The distraction for which Jud had prayed.

Not a trained professional after all, startled by the unanticipated intrusion, Julie glanced over her shoulder. The gun moved away from Cooper as she instinctively turned to meet the new threat.

In that instant, two gunshots ripped through the silence. One going wild; the other finding its mark.

The sharp smell of gunpowder and the booming echo of shots filtered down the hall and summoned help. Jud ran to Cooper where the child fell when he shot Julie between the eyes. She lay on the floor, eyes wide open, mouth in an astonished O and a neat thin line of blood flowing from her forehead down the side of her head. Jud kicked her still smoking gun away as he picked up Cooper. The boy wrapped his arms so tightly around his neck that Jud was in danger of suffocating.

Together they hurried to the bathroom. He pushed open the door and hollered, "Lottie!"

"Is it safe to come out now?" a weak voice asked. Lottie stuck her head around the stall door. When she saw Jud and Cooper were safe, she ran to them and threw her arms around Jud's waist. They reached for each other at the same time. Their kiss was soft and life affirming.

"I thought I'd die when I saw you open that door." Jud squeezed her, the little boy sandwiched between them.

Cooper objected. "You're squishing me!" He thumped Jud's shoulder.

"Sorry, little brother." He stepped aside while the doctor examined Julie, but never let go of Lottie as he told her his fear, then pride. "Then you came on out and yelled at her. Man, that took guts!" He noticed the terror she still carried in her expression. "You saved us."

"Actually, you saved us. I just distracted her. I've never seen a person pull and shoot a gun that fast. No wonder you wore camos today. You had that gun all along, didn't you?"

"Yes, tucked in the back of my blouse—just in case I needed it, but let's talk about it later. I see Ashley coming. She's going to want the story."

"Cooper Johnson! You scared me!"

"Hi, Mama. Miss Lottie saved me and Jud, and he shot a lady. Ain't that great?"

~ * ~

"Mom? You awake yet?" Jud leaned over the bed and brushed the dark hair off Mary's forehead.

"I am now that you shot up the place." Her weak answer set him to glowing.

"I was afraid you'd move and give away the game." He kissed her cheek.

One eye eased open, and the two stared at each other for a full moment.

"I love you, Mom."

"I love you, too, son." Mary started to drift off, sleep coming fast after the exertions of the last hour. "Will you walk me down the aisle,

Jud? Keenan expects you to."

"Sure will."

"In your uniform?"

"Yes, ma'am."

~ * ~

The Bleaker Police Department kept a tight lid on the multiple homicide cases.

Jud watched through a one-way glass in the police station. Jack Dansing sat on a hard chair in the interrogation room, leaning against the worn table. He had no clue what had happened in the hours he'd been there. Peter Dansing sat in a similar room next door.

A judge awakened before dawn issued a search warrant for the Dansing home. Before questioning either man, the officers wanted to search the home for weapons, in particular an old baseball bat, and illegal substances like steroids.

Officer Bell shoved the door open and came to stand beside Jud. "Damn, if we didn't find everything you said to look for. The bat was in the attic. I'd be willing to bet the lab will find traces of blood on it. Peter's room only looked innocent. Drugs were hidden in some pretty clever places throughout the house though. Lee found this." Bell held up a sack filled with bottles and loose pills.

"THG?" Jud was past being surprised by the Dansing family.

"That and Primobolan." When Jud raised an eyebrow, impressed by what the officer knew about the medicine, Bell blushed and admitted, "I looked it up on the computer on my way back to the station."

As they watched Jack, another man joined him.

"Wally Jenson. An attorney."

"How's this going down?" Jud couldn't take his eyes off the man on the other side of the glass.

"As far as Julie's death goes, you're cleared. That security camera you asked doc to install in Mary's room shows what happened and has Julie Dansing's confession for the murders of Mathew Jetter and Walter Vance." Bell swallowed hard at Walter's name. "She implicates

Jack for Jacob Longtree's murder and Peter for dealing. Lottie was an eyewitness to Julie trying to kidnap Cooper Johnson and attempting to shoot her." Bell shook his head. "Pillars of the community. That's how everyone saw the Dansing family. And they're nothing of the sort. Jack must have closed his eyes to what she was doing. And probably never questioned why Peter—or Walter for that matter—seemed to be so strong and bulked up. How blind can a man get?"

"He had enough on his conscience, I guess, without adding anyone else's problems." Jud nodded toward the interrogation room. "Can I...?"

"Sit in? I don't see why not. You can't speak directly to Jack though. Understood?"

They entered the room and took seats opposite the mayor and his lawyer.

"The officer that brought you here read you your Miranda rights. Is that correct, sir?" Bell opened a folder and pulled out his trusty pen.

"Yes, but I have no idea why I'm here."

"Sir, I must inform you of four things." Bell cleared his throat but didn't look to Jud for support. "First, your wife tried to murder Mary Longtree in her room at the hospital. Security cameras recorded her as she kidnapped little Cooper Johnson and held Sergeant Longtree hostage when she attempted to leave the hospital at gunpoint."

"What! This is absurd! Where's my wife? What kind of jackass stunt is this?" Jack jumped up from his chair, his face a vivid red. His body language and shocked expression suggested he had no idea his wife was capable of such action.

"Sit down!" Bell spoke in a calm firm voice and waited while Jack sat, though he still muttered about the very idea his wife could kill anyone. "Second, I must also inform you that while attempting to carry out the kidnapping, she was shot and killed."

"What...?" Jack Dansing seemed to wither into his chair like a balloon slowly losing air. "But...she just left to go to the store." His complexion went from red to deathly pale and then green. Jud reached for a trashcan and passed it over the table to the lawyer who eased it to Jack's side seconds before he got sick.

While the man threw up, Jud could tell Bell wanted to leave the room but didn't want to leave him alone with Dansing. "Need something, Officer?"

"Several bottled waters."

Jud pushed back his chair and left. When he returned, the foul smelling trashcan sat outside the door. He entered, passed the bottles to Bell and returned to his chair. He pushed one across the table to Jack.

"Who shot Julie?" Jack sat with his head down, his arms laid out across the table. He resembled a defeated man.

"Sergeant Longtree was forced to shoot when she not only threatened the boy but took a shot at Lottie Amberville."

"You! A no-good Injun! Just like your old man. Mean as a cut snake." Hatred poured out with every word. Jud recoiled, surprised that such venom could come from a man who seconds before had seemed so fragile.

Jack jumped up again and leaned over the table, reaching for Jud, but Bell was on him fast. His nightstick came down across Dansing's arms just hard enough to redirect his focus. He drew back his arms and rocked with them wrapped across this chest, pain evident in his eyes.

"Sit and answer the questions, Dansing. Or cool off in the tank." Bell shoved his stick toward Jack, promise in his expression and words.

The lawyer had said nothing during what he must have thought was an interview but was in fact an interrogation. He leaned over now, his arm across Jack's shoulders. "Drink some water, Jack, and let's hear what they have to say. But I warn you not to respond."

Jack nodded and swallowed half a bottle of water then sat up straighter in the chair. "You said four things. I hate to hear what the other two are."

While some might feel sorry for Jack for his loss of family, Jud felt nothing. Not even anger aimed at his father's murderer. Dansing just wasn't worth the effort. Life had moved on. He had learned how to deal with his loss. Would Dansing adjust? He doubted it.

"Third, your son has been implicated—by your late wife—as a drug dealer. Judge Hardy issued a warrant, and we obtained what we suspect are illegal steroids from Peter's room and your house. We also

137

found a list of dealers in Knoxville. Your wife apparently did the buying while Peter did the selling. He and Walter Vance. Mrs. Dansing is the one who killed Walter last night."

"Julie did what?" Dansing could barely speak; evidence against his family mounted by the moment. "Peter deals drugs?" He turned helplessly to his lawyer. "We can get him off, right? He's only a kid." The mayor never mentioned Walter.

"Peter is eighteen years old, sir. He'll stand trial as an adult." Bell closed one folder and opened the second one. "Finally, your wife implicated you in the bludgeoning death of Jacob Longtree. The warrant allowed us to look for the bat she said you kept. We have that in evidence now."

"But... But..." By now, Jack Dansing sputtered incoherently.

His lawyer came to his rescue. "What'll happen to Jack and Peter?"

"They'll stay here and be arraigned before Judge Hardy as soon as possible." Bell closed the folder and silently slid the pen into his pocket. "Bond will be set high. I doubt they'll be allowed to make bail...too much chance of a flight risk. Murder, drug possession and selling. Bleaker doesn't need people like that on the streets."

Wally Jenson looked as old as Jack now. He stood. "I need to be with Peter when you share all this. I assume he doesn't know about his mother or what his father is accused of."

Bell shook his head. "You're more than welcome to sit in on the interrogation. Dansing here doesn't need you tonight."

"And Officer, remember that these men are accused, not proven guilty. Until such time, they are suspects, not criminals."

Bell had the grace to look ashamed.

"Let's get this over with." The men cleared the room, and the bailiff took Jack to lockup.

But Bell called to Jud and motioned the lawyer on. "Sergeant, wait up a minute."

"What do you need, Bell?" Fatigue rode Jud hard. He wanted to see his mom and find Lottie.

"I saw that security video. Julie Dansing pushed that drug into your mom's IV. So how come it had no effect?"

"Part of the security plan. Not only did we set up a camera just in case, but the doctor also agreed to put her IV in her leg and hide the fluid bag. That IV in Mom's hand wasn't in her vein. The tape hid that. She was safe in that respect. If Cooper hadn't come along…" Because the boy did, Jud had tossed out Plan A and prayed for a Plan B. He still had no idea what that would have been.

~ * ~

Jud left the police station and walked the few blocks to the hospital. The spring morning resembled an early summer day, a bit warm for so early. On the way, he stepped into the diner.

"Have you seen Lottie Amberville this morning?" He didn't recognize the girl behind the cash register.

But she knew him. "No, Sergeant. But she stayed at Ashley's house last night. Probably sleeping late. If she comes in, want me to tell her you're looking for her?"

"Thanks. I'd appreciate that. But I'll probably see her first." He nodded then left.

He did find Lottie first, but not where he expected to see her. When he entered his mom's room, Lottie sat beside the bed. She looked beat up. Dragged out, bone tired. When she turned to him, she also looked hopeful.

Jud came straight to her, pulled her up and folded his arms around her. "I love you, lady. Never doubt it."

She let go a jagged little sigh, half way between crying and laughing, while she hugged him just as tightly. "I'm mad at you, remember."

"I know, sweetheart. I had to keep you safe. And I had to protect the evidence. I was going to tell you, but…"

"I still open my mouth before thinking. Right? No! Don't answer that. My ego can't take that right now, and my mind can't come back with a snappy reply." She stood on tiptoes and gave him a quick kiss.

"You two look good together. Now if I could just get you to…" Mary slumped back on her pillow. Fatigue still dragged her lovely features, but she looked better than she had since Mathew's murder.

Jud kissed her while he held Lottie's hand. "Hi, Mom. Feeling any better?"

"Some."

"Ready for the big event?"

"If the doctor will let me out of here," she grumbled while folding the sheet into a wad.

"Mom, you had a concussion, then surgery. You've been unconscious for a few days, too. Give the doc a break, will ya?" He grinned but caught Lottie's gasp and turned to find out what the problem was.

"I've never seen you do that!" Her grin was as big as his. "You are undeniably a very handsome man."

"For an Injun, as Vance would say."

"What the hell does he know? You're a handsome man no matter what color you are." Lottie moved into his arms again and cuddled there. "Nice," she whispered.

"Speaking of Vance and the police. Officer Bell came by earlier and took my statement. And I'd like to see Theo if I can." Mary sat up straighter in bed, ready to get up if Jud allowed.

"What exactly happened, Mom? That day?" Jud sat in the chair while Lottie sat on the edge of the bed, where Mary indicated.

"Mathew wanted me to help him come up with a plan for turning the drug evidence and the boys over to the law. I had to go to the bathroom, so stepped into the girls' dressing room. As I started out again, I saw someone with Mathew. They were arguing. The other person pushed him hard, and he fell against the bleacher. I could tell he was hurt bad. His head wound bled a lot on the floor. But instead of calling for help, the other person turned him on his stomach and struck a knife in his back! I was so scared my hand was shaking. The coffee in my cup sloshed, and I just knew she could hear me."

"She?"

"When she turned, she stepped into a patch of sunlight. Julie Dansing. She murdered Mathew and used your dad's knife to do it. I think I might have made a sound. She came toward me. I backed up and hid in the shower stall. I waited there for a long time. But she never came. When I got ready to leave, I guess I stepped in some more coffee I spilled. I was shaking pretty bad by then. Fell and cracked my head a good one. Woke up here." Mary's dark eyes welled with tears. "So much happened. Mathew and Walter gone. You and Lottie almost killed. Theo a broken man. The mayor and his son going to prison and Julie Dansing…Oh my…" Mary put a hand to her mouth, trying to stop the ugly words that seemed to come from her heart.

"It's over now, Mom. The law will take care of it. You only have to tell what you saw. No one's left in Mathew's case. It's only a matter of formality now. Lottie and I…" he squeezed her hand and gave her a sad tired smile, "we've got a lot of testifying to do." He leaned over and took his mother's hand. Lottie, Mary and he were connected. "We have a lot to look forward to. Good things. No one knows about them but you, Keenan and me. This will be something to lift the town's spirits."

"Everything's ready. Kept it all a secret, even from Lottie. Just waiting for the word." Mary's eyes sparkled. Jud thought she once again resembled the woman he remembered from his childhood.

"What's going on? What good things? I'm totally lost here!" Lottie laughed, but her humor sounded a bit frustrated.

Jud leaned over and kissed her. "We're having a wedding!"

Chapter Nine

Two funerals and a wedding, Jud thought. The stuff movies are made of. He approached the sheriff's house and stepped up on to a wide porch. Theo Vance sat in a rocker, his gaze off in the distance.

"Chief?" Jud saw no sign of recognition though he knew the man wasn't physically ill, only heart sick. "Chief Vance?"

Theo pulled himself back to the real world with difficulty, but at last he spotted Jud. "What do you want?"

His voice came out flat, not the usual Chief Vance at all. Skin pale and drawn, the man had gone through hell and come out the other side forever changed. Jud pitied him. No, not pity. He understood how losing a loved one hurt. How it numbed the mind for a long time. How time never really stopped the hurting. He understood what Theo Vance was going through.

"I came to say…" How did one say I'm sorry for your loss? "Walter was a good kid. He took a wrong turn somewhere but found the right way to go at the end. You would have been proud of his decision to straighten out his life. He loved you. That's why he wanted to help us."

Jud couldn't stay. Couldn't watch the police chief wither before his eyes. Grow old in the space of a few heartbeats. "I came home to walk my mom down the aisle at her wedding. I never meant to hurt anyone." Did the world unravel because he returned? Jud had asked himself that question more than once since Julie Dansing's death.

"Wasn't your fault. Walter…and the others…made their choices."

Vance spoke so low that Jud strained to hear. "Would have come to a head sooner or later. Walter might not have made such a good choice then. But..." Tears on the old man's cheeks tore at Jud's heart. This wasn't right. To lose and grieve and have no one. "But I loved him so much. And...I miss him."

"Yes, sir. I know. Walter's gone, but these folks still need you. Maybe you can help some other kid find the right way to live. Learn from Walter's mistake. I hope so." What else could he say? Words wouldn't heal Vance's wounded heart...only time could ease the pain.

"I have to go now, sir. Maybe I can come back and visit again?" He had no idea if Vance would want that, but Jud couldn't leave the man alone like this.

"Come if you want." That sounded more like the chief he remembered. "And..." he sighed, "tell Mary I'm happy for her."

~ * ~

Mom's wedding is beyond the ordinary, Jud thought, as he adjusted the sash at his waist. Lottie was Mary's bridesmaid. Keenan Waverly, as the groom, asked Jud to be best man. So Jud, minus hat and sword, would escort Lottie to the altar, then return back up the aisle to his mom. Meanwhile Keenan would come out to stand with the Cherokee pastor. Finally, in full dress uniform complete with ceremonial sword, he would escort the bride to the altar, then step to the side and become best man. He shook his head. As he'd told Lottie and Keenan, "No one but Mom could come up with a plan like this."

Lottie, Ashley and other friends had decorated the church with wild flowers. Neither Mary nor Keenan wanted music. Though only a week had passed since Mary's release from the hospital, in that time she had invited practically the whole town to the wedding. The school superintendent offered the high school cafeteria for the reception. In the end, friends took care of food and drink. All her family had to do was sit back, relax and show up at the church.

In the small room to one side of the church lobby, Jud paced nervously. Lottie stepped out of the second room. "You ready?" He finally focused on her. "Man, you look great!" Her sky blue dress hugged her body and made her dark eyes even darker. She wore the necklace and earrings Mary had given her, the ones that Jud had designed for his mom. "Your hair is beautiful." His hand slid down her back, caressing the wavy mass.

"And you're most handsome, sir." Lottie gathered a small bouquet of flowers and a striped blanket that she folded over her arm. "Ready."

They stepped into the small lobby, before the open double doors leading into the sanctuary. Every row in the church looked full. Eyes straight ahead, they slow marched down the aisle in total silence. Jud left her at the side of the steps, turned and walked back to the lobby.

Once there, he watched Keenan and Able Whitewing, the Cherokee pastor, enter and take their positions. When everyone was in place, he stepped into the bride's room. He set his cap squarely on his head and belted his sword around his waist. Satisfied with the results, he picked up a colorful blanket similar to the one Lottie carried. Opening the second door, he called softly, "It's time, Mom."

Never had he seen his mother so beautiful. Her vibrant blue dress accented her deep tinted skin. Her eyes glowed with excitement. She wore jewelry just like Lottie's; for Mary, a symbol of her heritage. A loose bouquet of wild flowers shook ever so slightly in her small hands. But she came to Jud and stopped him when he would have held out his arm for her.

"Jud, I want to say something before we leave." She waited patiently when he would have shushed her. "I loved your father with every fiber of my being. Losing him almost killed my heart and soul. Time lessened the pain but not the memory. Keenan slipped quietly into my life. And soon I found that my day was not complete without him. While the memory of Jacob is sweet, life with Keenan will be just as sweet. I ask your blessings today."

"Aw, Mom. Now why did you have to do that?" Though Jud smiled and joked, he wiped off the tears he saw gathering on her lashes. "You'll ruin your makeup." He pulled her arm through his. "I love you, and I respect Keenan and welcome him into our family. Dad would be pleased to see you in love again. He'd be the first to tell you this is the right thing. I'm saying it for both of us. It's the right thing. Keenan's a fine man. And speaking of him, we're keeping him waiting." He tugged her arm.

Love and pride almost set Jud's heart to bursting as he walked his mother down the aisle that day. So much had happened since he'd come back home. Awful things. But tucked among those agonizing events were special ones. During that long walk, he caught Keenan's eyes but remained straight-faced. Somewhere among the crowd, he heard Cooper say in a stage whisper, "Mama, look at my brother. He's purdy!" Ashley's sigh was almost as loud. He remained straight-faced. But when he saw Lottie, he broke out in a smile that matched the groom's.

Solemnly he maneuvered his mom next to Keenan, waited for Pastor Whitewing to ask who gave the woman. Replied and gave her hand to the bridegroom. With that done, his part was almost over. He stepped back to the side and listened to the rest of the ceremony, glad that his ancestors were as involved as the rest of them.

In the smooth flowing language of Mary's ancestors, Cherokee Pastor Whitewing spoke. *"Great Spirits. Cherokee Fathers. Your daughter Mary has come to ask for this man Keenan Waverly. A good man. A strong provider. He accepts Mary. A good woman. A foundation for his home. They represent balance and all that is good in loving each other."* He repeated his words in English.

In Cherokee again. *"Do you, Mary, take this man Keenan as your husband? To have and hold in all manner of life from now until your death?"*

She repeated the question in English for Keenan's sake then answered in both Cherokee and English: "I do."

The pastor repeated the question to Keenan, and he replied in English: "I do."

"The rings, please." Lottie handed over a thick ring while Jud handed over a smaller more delicate one. "The rings symbolize unending love and devotion." Keenan slipped Mary's on her finger, and she did the same with his.

"According to Keenan's culture, this man and woman have satisfied the law and church. Mary's culture asks one more thing."

Keenan reached back to Jud who handed him the somber hued blanket. Then he turned to Mary and pulled her nearer. She held out her arms, and he laid the blanket across them. "I will love you until I pass from this world. This blanket will warm you like that love." From his pocket, he pulled out a small piece of dried venison. Laying it on top of the blanket, he added, "I will provide safety, shelter and food for you and our family." His kiss sealed his vow.

Mary exchanged her bouquet and his gifts for the blanket Lottie held out. Like Keenan, she draped it across his arms. "Receive this blanket as a symbol of my love and devotion. We will live warm beneath its shelter." Turning back to Lottie, she pulled several long berry stems out of her bouquet. Placing them on the blanket, she vowed, "I will gather all things good and make a home filled with peace and calm for you and our family." She kissed him but lingered long enough to make Keenan smile.

Mary draped Keenan's blanket over her arm and carried the flowers and venison. Keenan folded Mary's gift over his arm and held the berry stems. Together they faced the pastor. *"Fathers of our ancestors, welcome Keenan Waverly into your tribe. Walk with Mary and Keenan as they pass through their lives."* He repeated his prayer in English then added, "According to Cherokee tradition and by the authority invested in me by the State of South Carolina, I now pronounce you man and wife." He turned Mary and Keenan to the church, waited while she took his arm then addressed the audience. "Ladies and gentlemen, may I present Mr. and Mrs. Keenan Waverly."

Despite the gravity of the ceremony, the church now exploded in applause. Mary burst into tears but let them flow as she laughed with Keenan who, like Jud did earlier, gently wiped them off his wife's face. Together they made a short journey of the trip back down the aisle. Jud escorted Lottie behind them.

Bride, groom, attendants and friends burst forth into a picture perfect spring day.

~ * ~

Jud swayed to the rhythm of the music, Lottie tucked neatly in his arms. Next to them the bride and groom danced. Others crowded around them on the dance floor.

"I've got five years left in the Marines before I retire." He eyed Lottie to see what her reaction would be.

"Really?" She spoke casually as if his words meant nothing special. But he saw her interest.

"I want to come back here." He pulled her tighter.

"What're you going to do when you get here?"

"Give Theo Vance a run for his money. Be the next police chief." Jud figured that ought to get her attention.

"Jud! That's a great idea." Lottie pressed her lips to his. "But is that really a good reason to return to Bleaker?" Mischief twinkled in her dark eyes now.

"Well, Mom and Keenan are here." He shrugged, unsure for once what to do next.

"And?"

"You're gonna make me ask, aren't you?" His sigh fluffed her hair.

"I thought I would. I'd like to hear it. At least once." She had control and knew it. No matter how Jud would have loved not making a fool of himself, she was going to make him ask. She had used that creativity of hers to focus on one thing: him.

In the middle of the dance, he stopped. Why was he worried? He wanted to ask. So get it over.

"Lottie, would you marry me when I return to Bleaker? Even if I don't become police chief?"

"You returned with honor once," she said, using his own words, "you can do it again." She drew his head down to hers and reached for his lips. Before she kissed him, Lottie whispered, "And I'll be waiting."

About the Author

In humid beautiful Texas one hundred miles from the Gulf of Mexico, I have been an educator, Challenge Course facilitator, photographer, security staff and now a writer. Wife, mother and grandmother. These titles fit me well. I've held them all--some far longer than others. The title I long strived for was that of writer--now published author.

As a writer, my imagination creates whatever I want. Once I've written something I want to share, it is time to edit, hone that manuscript until there is no doubt what I want the reader to experience. I'm still working at that. And always will. Any writer who says, "I've got this down pat," is only fooling herself.

There are no rules to what your imagination comes up with, but there are guidelines to follow if you want that story to be the best it can. So writers are also learners. Constantly attending conferences, taking classes, reading, communicating with fellow writers. The trick is to take what you learn and make it your own. Write in a way that no one else does. Be fresh!

There is no new story--each has been told. The idea is to tell your story in a new way. So we fill notebooks with ideas, pages with storybook names, jot down dire circumstances then one day, we the writers, pull out an idea from here and a name from there and put it all together. We add tension, conflict, danger, doubt, suspense and maybe love if that's your thing. Polish the words and craft them until you have a story that begs to be read and enjoyed.

That is my challenge: to write such a story. I strive toward that goal every day. Enjoy....Jane Carver (also writing as Elizabeth Eden and Ruth Bolin)

http://janiecarver2011@wordpress.com

Other Books by Jane Carver with Melange Books, LLC

Fairy Tears

Western Ways
Winning The Ranger's Heart

Until I'm Safe, a young adult novel, writing as Jane Grace

Coming Soon!

Ghosts In My Soul, a young adult novel, writing as Jane Grace

www.ingramcontent.com/pod-product-compliance
Lightning Source LLC
Chambersburg PA
CBHW051837170626
46807CB00003B/1218